BACULUM

BOOK FOUR OF THE ANGELBOUND LINCOLN SERIES

CHRISTINA BAUER

COPYRIGHT

Monster House Books
Brighton, MA 02135
ISBN 9781946677488
First Edition

DEDICATION

**For All Those Who Kick Ass, Take Names
and Read Books**

CONTENTS

COLLECTED WORKS

Angelbound Lincoln

The Angelbound experience as told by Prince Lincoln

1. Duty Bound
2. Lincoln
3. Trickster
4. Baculum
5. Angelfire

Angelbound Offspring

The next generation takes on Heaven, Hell, and everything in between

1. Maxon
2. Portia
3. Zinnia

4. Rhodes

5. Kaps

6. Mack

7. Huntress

Angelbound Origins

About a quasi (part demon and part human) girl who loves kicking butt in Purgatory's Arena

1. Angelbound

2. Scala

3. Acca

4. Thrax

5. The Dark Lands

6. The Brutal Time

7. Armageddon

8. Quasi Redux

9. Clockwork Igni

Fairy Tales of the Magicorum

Modern fairy tales with sass, action, and romance

1. Wolves and Roses

2. Moonlight and Midtown

3. Shifters and Glyphs

4. Slippers and Thieves

5. Bandits and Ball Gowns

6. Fire and Cinder

7. Fairies and Frosting

8. Towers and Tithes

9. Evil Queens and Goblin Kings

Dimension Drift

Dystopian adventures with science, snark, and hot aliens

1. Scythe

2. Umbra

3. Alien Minds

4. ECHO Academy

5. Justice

6. Slate

Pixieland Diaries

About sassy pixie Calla and her love-crush-nemesis, the elf prince Dare

1. Pixieland Diaries

2. Calla

3. Dare

4. Winter Prince

5. Ley Queen

Beholder

Where a medieval farm girl discovers necromancy and true love

1. Cursed

This is a finished series.

Dear Readers,

Get ready for the Viking Games! BACULUM turned out to be such a trip and I'm super excited to share it with you. Here are some key points to consider before you get started.

Point One. There's A Dual Point of View

Myla and Lincoln's voices are back in this novel!!! The core conflict just wouldn't work unless readers got to know both their inner thoughts. Plus, it's fun to write.

That said, the story is very much centered in Lincoln's world and his character arc, so get ready for a deeper view into the inner workings of our favorite Mister the Prince.

Point Two. This Takes Place Both Before And After ACCA

Please note that this book also takes place after the events of ACCA (Angelbound Origins Book #3). There are no spoilers here if you read out of order. I also wrote it so you can enjoy it as a stand alone. That said, to set this story up, I go back to Lincoln and Myla's past. When you read it, I hope it all makes sense.

Point Three. What Is My Problem?

At this point you may wonder: why do I write things out of sequence? Wasn't ACCA published a while ago?

Here's my honest answer: *I have no idea.*

This is just how my gift works. I know it's different from everyone else, and sometimes Business-Me wants to take Author-Me out and kick my own ass, if that makes sense. But then I drink coffee and get back to writing. Self-distraction is a very useful skill.

Enough of my preamble, let's get to the Angelbound fun. I hope you enjoy BACULUM!

CB

BACULUM

YEARS AGO

LINCOLN
SIXTEENTH BIRTHDAY

1 1:58 p.m.

11:59 p.m.

Midnight.

And my sixteenth birthday is officially here!

Some folks might celebrate with cake and presents. In my family, we hunt demons.

I know. Awesome.

Father and I march through Brazil's largest vine forest, Mata de Cipó. In every direction, long sheets of woody tendrils sway around us. Father and I are tracking a vitis, which is a snake-like demon. There's no rain. Winds are low. A full moon casts everything in pale light.

Perfect conditions for a hunt.

Suddenly, an electric sense of alarm rips through my nervous system. Something watches us…. and it's close.

I picture things through my enemy's eyes. The vitis would begin by spotting two figures in dark body armor. Next it would notice Father's white hair and barrel chest. I'd appear younger, leaner, and much easier to kill.

Most likely, the demon will attack me first.

Suddenly, a nearby vine drifts away from the breeze. My pulse speeds. Moving slowly, I angle my head for a better view. Sure enough, that lone tendril is covered in a grid of black dots. Only a vitis has skin like that.

Father sees the danger, same as I do. He raises his fist twice. It's a hand signal that means, *Do you want me to attack?*

I shake my head. *No, I've got his.*

Battle energy spikes through me. The demon's wiry arm slowly twists nearer. A few inches from my throat, it stops.

Up close, I can see how each dark point on the creature's skin holds a single needle. *That's definitely a vitis.* I've never fought these before, but I know their needles inject neurotoxins. If I get enough in my bloodstream, I'll be unconscious in seconds.

In other words, once the battle starts, I must take down this vitis and fast.

On it.

Reaching into my holster, I pull out my baculum, which are a pair of silver rods that create different angelfire weapons. As I picture the blade I need, the two bars ignite into a dagger made from white flame. Reaching forward, I angle the fiery blade toward the demon's arm.

Somewhere in the sheet of vines, the main part of the vitis lets out a low hiss.

Clearly, I've got its attention now. Best to announce my purpose.

"I am Lincoln Vidar Osric Aquilus, High Prince of the Thrax. According to human news reports, a massive snake has been bothering nearby villages. Stealing livestock. Ruining fences. Almost killing a child. If this is your doing, then you must return to Hell now. I have a magical charm which will keep you there forever."

At this point, most demons would slink away.

Not this one.

Instead, the rest of the creature oozes out behind from the wall of vines. Like a coil of wire, the monster's green tentacles stack up, one on top of each other. Within seconds, the ropes take on a humanoid shape. The creature sports empty pits for eyes and a dark slit of a mouth. Its tentacle arm still hovers just above my skin.

"I am innocent," says the vitis.

"Let's see," I state.

With my left fist, I keep my angelfire dagger angled toward the tentacle-arm. Using my free hand, I pull a quarter from my pocket.

"This is no regular coin," I declare. "You're looking at a truth charm."

By the way, thrax always conceal their magical items as everyday objects. If we lose a few—which happens more than it should—then humans don't know what they've found.

I speak directly into the coin. "Has this demon terrorized humans?"

A warm awareness moves through my veins. Since I'm part angel, this heat comes from the charm's magic mixing with my supernatural nature.

White flame erupts from the coin. *Angelfire.* This doesn't burn me, but it does summon Heavenly power. Hundreds of angelic voices speak at once. Their tones are so lively and musical, it's almost enough to distract me from the vitis.

Almost, but not quite.

"Guilty, guilty, guilty," sings the chorus.

"That settles it," I declare. "The angels have spoken. You must leave for Hell. This is your last warning."

The vitis howls. "Never! Die, demon fighter!"

We thrax have rules. One is to never attack unless

directly threatened. In this case, just poking a tentacle near my face doesn't count as a full-on assault.

But the words *die, demon fighter?* That definitely checks the *attack box*. And things get worse from there.

Fast as a whip, the demon's tentacle-arm loops around my throat. Hundreds of tiny needles dig into my neck. Each pricker burns my skin as it releases neurotoxin. If I don't do something quickly, I'll be paralyzed under the demon's grip.

To fully kill a vitis, I must combine two potions. In one swift movement, I reset my baculum while pulling a pair of vials from different pockets on my body armor. Meanwhile, the neurotoxin spreads through my bloodstream. My head turns woozy.

I smash the vials between my palms. A small cloud of black smoke rises. The demon's grip on my neck tightens. Now I can add *lack of oxygen* to my list of problems.

High-pitched ringing fills my ears. Through the noise, I vaguely hear Father's voice. "Lincoln, are you all right?"

The mists of the two vials swirl together, but they don't combust. I know these potions can take a few seconds to work, but this seems extreme. My legs turn wobbly beneath me.

Finally, flames erupt all around the vitis. The creature lets out a high-pitched screech before crumbling into ash.

The world around me gets even more blurry. While forcing myself to stay upright, I reach into my pocket, pull out a stick of gum, and pop it into my mouth. This is no ordinary treat but another thrax charm. As I chew, a healing spell gets released. Within moments, my mind is clear and my body's back to normal. I straighten my stance and exhale.

My father steps to my side. "All better, son?"

"Yes."

He pats my shoulder. "Well done. Happy birthday to you, indeed!"

"Thank you. Any suggestions?"

"Oh, it's been years since I could teach you anything about demon fighting." He sighs. "If only your mother could have seen that."

Normally, my mother, Octavia, joins all my birthday patrols. This year, she's on a demon hunting safari to find monsters in less-protected regions. Sadly, she's uncovered a serious infestation and must stay longer than expected. I told her that I'd consider it a great birthday present if she destroyed tons of evil for me.

"Once your mother returns, I'll share every second of that battle with her." He beams. "We're both so proud of the man you're becoming."

Father and I share a smile. My heart lightens. A memory appears. I recall toddling around with my first wooden sword while Father cheers on every swipe I make through the air. Looking back, I can draw a direct line from that instance to this battle. Sometimes, being an only child means a lot of pressure. Right now, it brings me nothing but joy.

Rustling erupts in the nearby vines, breaking up my thoughts. Birds caw as they take to the air. Monkeys chatter warnings. Something approaches, only it's not a careful predator like the vitis. Kneeling, I set my fingertips against the soft ground. Telltale vibrations move up my arm.

Father tilts his head. "What is it?"

A few minutes ago, Father's face was tight with concern over the vitis demon. At this point, he seems downright casual as he asks about the newcomer. No question what this means.

Father already knows who's on the way.

"Someone's marching through the vines." I rise to stand. "And they're disturbing everything in their path."

"Oh, my." Father blinks innocently. "Who could that be?"

"I believe you already know."

Father winks. "You've got me there."

My bet? Our surprise visitor is none other than

Aldred, the Earl of Acca and the official poster boy for *bag of dicks syndrome*. Aldred is selfish, rude, and my father's personal stalker.

"Ringmaster Kell is on his way," states Father.

I take a half-step backward. *That's unexpected.*

Kell runs the Viking Games, where father-son teams fight Norse monsters in a massive arena. It's all part of a rare phenomenon called a Salient, where a chunk of one reality gets stuck in another. In this case, a bit of the Norse Universe lodged into our own.

Tapping my chin, I consider Kell's visit. The ringmaster is a dark elf mage from the Norse Universe. If Father's inviting the him here, then Kell must offer the thrax some kind of advantage.

A realization appears.

"The Viking Arena is built on the Purple Salient," I say slowly. "That land comes from another reality. No one sets foot on that soil without Kell's magical approval. Such a place could make a nice *safe zone* for our people. No demons. Lots of entertainment. Perhaps Kell will give us some land... for the right price."

Father chuckles. "Exactly!"

Before us, the wall of vines shimmies and parts. Through the break in the tendrils, waves of green mist pour into the small clearing. A fresh chill crawls up my spine as my inner angelic power responds to this new magic.

For the record, I liked the warm sensation from the truth charm much better. There's something unsettling about getting a chill in the middle of a tropical zone.

Placing the back of his hand by his mouth, Father speaks in a low and conspiratorial tone. "Kell's a real showman. Consider yourself warned."

The green haze solidifies into a kind of curtain before us. Transparent skulls swirl within this emerald sheet. Mystical drumbeats fill the air. A sickly-sweet smell rises.

Talk about making an entrance. Father wasn't kidding.

Kell steps through the mist and into the clearing. Since he's a dark elf, Kell has green skin, pointed ears, and a flat face. Scrolls hang from his belt, along with a single skull. Lines of power twist across his exposed flesh.

"Behold, I am Ringmaster Kell, Ruler of the Purple Salient and Leader of the Viking Games."

My supernatural shiver turns even more arctic. After years of demon patrol, I know exactly what that means.

No matter what titles Kell may give himself, this guy's a predator, pure and simple.

KELL

2

LINCOLN

*R*ingmaster Kell puffs up his chest. Behind him, transparent skulls spin along his newly-created sheet of mist. Some of the heads seem to be laughing. It's creepy beyond reason.

"Speak, boy!" he commands.

Prince or not, I don't appreciate random orders from strangers. So I give Kell what humans would call a *golfer's clap*.

"Excellent entrance," I say smoothly.

In response, Kell shoots me an angry glare. Clearly, he's used to a far more enthusiastic response.

Father applauds as well, although with much more vigor.

Kell glares at the pile of ash that was once a vitis

demon. "You took down the father. Yet you missed the son."

The ringmaster lifts his arms. Tendrils of emerald smoke twist out from his clawed fingers. The misty cords reach into a nearby wall of vines and pull out a small vitis. Like the first creature, this one is humanoid and made from stacked cords. The big difference is how the new vitis is a child. There's no missing its small stature.

What happens next only takes a matter of seconds. Still, each moment moves slowly in my mind. Kell opens his mouth. A fresh tendril of green smoke flies out from his tongue to slam into the vitis. The little creature instantly erupts into flame, screeching as it burns into ash.

Anger rises inside me. I round on Kell. "That is not an honorable fight. You attacked a lesser foe who showed no aggression."

"But I am not thrax," declares Kell. "In my world, fathers determine their son's fate. And if a parent dies prematurely? Then their child has no right to live."

My father nods. "We thrax have similar values, only we show it in different ways." He looks to me. "Isn't that right, Lincoln?"

I fold my arms over my chest. "Death is far different

from helping your royal parent determine new trade routes."

"You need to understand the rules of the Norse Universe," states Kell. "Come see my Viking Games for yourself. I'll even give you free tickets."

I rub my neck and consider Kell's offer. If there is a chance to find a safe zone for my people, then I need to look into it.

"What do you say?" asks Father. "Will you check it out?"

I nod. "Definitely."

Kell grins. "Then I'll see you at 8 p.m. tonight."

Raising his arms, the ringmaster sets loose a fresh round of mist. Within seconds, another green haze appears. This time, the cloud is so heavy, I can only see a few inches in front of me.

Kell's voice echoes in my mind. *Maybe you'll join the games yourself as one of our warriors. Think upon it.*

The haze slowly fades. When it's completely vanished, Ringmaster Kell is gone as well.

I look to Father. "Did you hear what Kell said?"

"Yes, the games start at 8 p.m." Father frowns. "I can't join, sadly. I have a solid waste committee meeting. Being king isn't all fun and games, you know."

"So you didn't hear Kell say anything else?"

Father shakes his head. "Why, did you?"

"He asked me to join the games as a warrior."

"Oh, he's just being showy, I'm sure. When you attend tonight, be sure to check if it's a suitable refuge for our kind. If you like the idea of a safe zone in the Purple Salient, then I'll start negotiations."

"Will do."

As I think upon the encounter with Kell, I'm left with the unsettling feeling of having just lost a competition that I didn't notice having joined.

Not a pleasant sensation at all.

3

MYLA

FIFTEEN

*I*t's not my birthday, but it might as well be.

Case in point. For my last actual birthday, my biggest gift turned out to be *early onset curves*. Turns out, having extra boobs certainly helps me during arena battles (let's just say male opponents get easily distracted) but there are negatives as well. For instance, try finding a good bra in Purgatory. Total pain in the tits.

But back to my most recent birthday. Mom gifted me some not-so-gently-used sweatpants along with a card that read:

I love you, but I hate how our ghoul overlords make you fight in Purgatory's Arena.

Don't die, birthday girl!

Mom wishes that I *not-die* daily, so that bit was no shocker. As for the sweatpants, I was amazed Mom found used stuff at all. So it wasn't the crappiest birthday ever. That said, what's happening tonight is sooooooo much better. I'm about to enjoy the most amazing gift: an evening of me, my buddy Walker, and the Viking Games.

Can't wait.

I even borrowed a cute outfit from my best friend Cissy for the occasion. This is huge stuff. I am not Dressy Girl.

By the way, you'd think Cissy would beg to join me at the games, but my bestie is totally disinterested. She says she doesn't like watching stuff die. Whatever. I offered to cover her eyes during the gross parts, but that didn't help.

To each their own, I guess.

Cissy aside, there's still one major hurdle standing between me and tonight's fun. In order to reach the games, I must first get past my uber-anxious mother.

That won't be easy.

Over the years, I've mastered the over-protective parental mind. Mom thinks that if I attend the Viking Games, it'll only encourage my so-called *reckless nature*.

Meh. There's not much more 'reck' for me to get 'less' of, if you know what I mean.

Long story short, I told Mom that I'm fighting in *Purgatory's* Arena tonight. Not a word has been said about Vikings and Norse whatnot. With any luck, Mom won't remember that Purgatory never even has night matches... Or notice how I'm wearing a cute outfit instead of my usual sweats... Or-or detect my crappy lying skills.

Am I proud of myself for fibbing to Mom? Absolutely not. Will I do it for the Viking Games? Hells, yeah. Half my class at Purgatory High has already seen them at least once.

Which brings me to the present moment. I sit at my chipped Formica kitchen table in our dingy ranch house in Lower Purgatory. Like most meals, it's just me and Mom. I don't have siblings, and my father's identity remains a big question mark. Mom knows who he is, but she insists that I never ask.

So I bug her about it all the time.

One of these days, Mom will crack and give me a name. I have massive amounts of faith in my ability to nudge someone into submission.

But now is not the time for a *who's my daddy* battle. Instead, I pretend to be interested in the ghoul-made pile of slop on my plate. Mom stands by the sink while pinning me with a worried stare.

Basically, I'm a younger version of her. We both have long auburn hair, lots of curves and a long tail that's covered in dragonscales. Sadly, we're total opposites in the personality department. Mom's capacity for adventure falls somewhere between a large rock and your average house plant. Meanwhile, I kill demons for fun and avoid school like a boss. It's a recipe for drama, especially at mealtimes.

Speaking of which, Mom keeps staring at my plate. "You're not eating," she says.

To look busy, I push little chunks of mystery meatloaf around until they make a smiley face.

"Don't play with your dinner," warns Mom. "This is a new type of frozen meal from our gracious ghoul overlords." She steps closer. "How does it taste?"

"Not sure yet." I lift my fork to my nose and inhale. The scent of dead fish fills my nasal cavity. "Smells nasty."

"Walker will be here soon. You must eat something. "

Walker is both a ghoul and my honorary older brother. I fight in Purgatory's Arena and—lucky me—it's Walker's job to transport my butt around. Tonight, he'll sneak me off to the Viking Games.

Mom sighs. "Just one bite, Myla."

"But there's something *in this.*" I take a closer look at the gray slop on my fork and, dammit, I'm totally right. "Check it out." I lift my utensil. "Is that an eyeball or what?"

Mom shoots a quick glance my way. "That is not an eyeball." The words come out as more of a question, though.

"Sha." I raise the fork even higher. "That could totally be a little fish eyeball. Plus, I saw the package before you tossed it in the trash. How can you trust something called *Mystery Loaf Supreme?*"

On a side note, I don't believe that the words *baby, back* or *loaf* should ever be used in conjunction with naming a meal.

Mom lets out another sigh. "You must eat, honey."

"I'll be fine. Besides, I can grab something at the games."

The moment I speak the words *grab something at the games,* I want to face-palm myself.

Mom pales. "What do you mean, *grab something?* They don't serve food at Purgatory's Arena."

In my mind, I picture a big red light flashing just above Mom's head, along with a computerized voice saying, *ten seconds to maternal meltdown.* I slap on a smile and try to redirect the conversation.

"Demons enjoy meals sometimes," I begin. "Like last month, I killed this slimy globulus monst—"

"And another thing," interrupts Mom. "Purgatory has *matches,* not *games.* You fight evil souls to keep them out of Heaven. That is *not* entertainment." Mom rounds the table to stare at me face-on. "What are you *really* up to?"

At this moment, I reach a crossroads. There are three ways I could work this.

One, I could make up a lie. That's a crap choice because I am supremely awful at fibbing.

With door number two, I jam this gray goop into my head and pretend my mouth is full. Mom will then wait a full two minutes so I don't choke while I eat.

Still. Eyeballs. Eew.

Which leaves option number three. This selection involves moving more eyeball slop around on my plate. Sadly, this is a crap plan because it only buys me about three seconds before the aforementioned Momular meltdown.

"Myla," says Mom in a warning tone. "I know when you're scheming. Tell me everything."

Suddenly, a low hum sounds. I block the desire to cheer my lungs out. This particular noise means that a ghoul portal is about to open.

Walker is almost here.

Unlike me, my honorary older brother is a totally

smooth liar. He's also the one with tickets to the Viking Games, so there's that, too.

Sure enough, a tall rectangular shape appears by the far wall. A man in dark robes steps through the portal.

Yay, Walker!

As a ghoul, Walker's appearance froze at the moment he died. He now looks to be twenty-something with pale skin, a brush cut and sideburns. Like all ghouls, Walker wears long black robes with loopy sleeves.

"Greetings." Walker stares at my plate and gasps. "*What* are you eating?" The way he says the word *what*, it's like my plate is covered in poison. Which, let's face it, it probably is.

"Ghoul mystery loaf," I reply. Then I hold up my fork, taking care to angle it so the suspected eyeball is visible.

Thus begins what I like to call a Dual Maternal Distraction. Not only has Walker appeared in our kitchen—which is a great way to derail Mom's Worry Train—but he's also circling the conversation back to my ghoul-made meal. Beautiful.

"Help me, Walker," pleads Mom. "Myla must eat something."

"Not. That." Walker scoops up my plate. After crossing the room, he scrapes the eyeball-slurry into the trash. Next Walker reaches into the loopy sleeves of his ghoul robes, pulls out a handful of Demon Bars, and tosses them in my direction.

Best honorary brother ever.

I catch one bar in my right hand and the other in my left. Meanwhile, my tail pops up and grabs the third.

Mom frowns at me. "Demon Bars are not a meal."

"Yeth they are," I say through a mouthful of choco-latey goodness. I scan the wrapper to offer up a few helpful ingredients as evidence. "It says here that Demon Bars are packed with psychocholoro-something and monosodium superscience."

Mom gives me the side eye. "That's not helping your case. At least, the *ghoul eyeball loaf* was a warm meal."

"Ha!" I point at Mom's nose. "So you admit there was an eyeball!"

Walker gives me the barest head shake. The meaning is clear. *Drop the eyeball shtick, Myla. Let me get to work.*

I lean back in my chair and mime zipping my mouth shut. *Make it happen, buddy.*

Walker refocuses on Mom. "What about you, Camilla? Where's your dinner?"

Like every ghoul, Walker has all-black eyes. Only unlike the rest of his fellow undead, Walker's peepers are super big and soulful. Plus, the man knows how to work them like a pro. Take this moment, for example. Walker gives Mom a look that's all concerned and watery. It's as if the world will stop spinning if she doesn't snack soon.

And that's how the magic happens.

As Walker does his sad-eye routine, Mom's worry about what I'm *truly up to* vanishes. I'd say it's a coincidence, but there's no such thing when it comes to Walker. The man is a maestro of manipulation.

"I'll find something to eat later," says Mom. "Myla comes first."

Walker reaches into his other sleeve and pulls out a small cup that's marked *freeze-dried chicken and ramen.* He offers her the container. "You always liked these."

Mom's face brightens. "This is from before the ghouls took over Purgatory. I didn't know any were left."

Walker winks. "I have my sources."

Once more, I hit a crossroads. In one direction, there's the evening of warrior fun at the Viking Games. But the opposite path might be far more interesting.

I'm talking about this *ramen soup revelation.*

Mom never talks about her past... or who my father really is. The fact that she used to chow down on ramen noodles? That's huge news. Freeze-dried stuff is the meal of choice for someone who's knee-deep in work. I wasn't around when Mom was a noodle hound, so what was she busy with, exactly? The undeadlies weren't running things yet, so it's not like she had her current job of mending ghoul robes.

Every cell in my body wants to push for answers. Another key consideration is the fact that I've finished all my Demon Bars, so I can really drive my points home without worrying about stuff like chewing.

I raise my pointer finger and open my mouth, ready to unleash my verbal Kraken.

Walker glide-walks to stand right between me and Mom. The sneak now blocks my line of sight, which in turn throws off any Mom-related attacks.

A heavy tension fills the air. In essence, Walker and I transform into gunslingers straight out of the human's Old West. Both of us have ideas about what happens tonight, and there's only room in this town for one of our concepts. Walker takes the first shot in our verbal battle.

"Ready for the *arena*?" Walker puts extra emphasis on the word *arena*, which means he's reminding me of our real goal for the evening, the Viking Games.

I tap my chin. "I've been thinking."

Translation: I really want to yell at Mom about ramen noodles.

Walker steps closer. He's crazy-tall and uses that height to his advantage. "But *I'm* the one portaling you around."

Translation, part two: I hate being in the middle of your father fights. And without me, you'd never leave this house to go anywhere.

Needless to say, the tumbleweeds roll by, I reset my verbal six shooter, and Walker wins this standoff in a big way.

I hop up. "Let's hit it."

Walker sighs. "Thank you."

MYLA

4

LINCOLN

*A*fter Kell leaves, Father and I hike to the nearest Pulpitum transfer station. The after-realms are made up of Heaven with angels, Hell with demons, the Dark Lands with ghoul-kind, Purgatory with quasis, and Antrum with thrax. Our home lies deep beneath the Earth's surface. Pulpitum are a secret network of magical platforms that move my people around.

As we hike to the station, I ask Father about the Viking Games. Sadly, he's more interested in discussing how the Earl of Acca wants me to marry one of his daughters. Needless to say, I've become an expert at ignoring these betrothal talks.

So I don't listen as we march to the transfer station.

I continue to tune out the wedding pleas as we make the magical ride to Antrum.

And once the journey is over, I act as if Father has stopped blabbing about possible brides altogether. I say my goodbyes and simply walk away. Over the years, I've found that when Father gets in a marriage-mood, the best approach is to make a quick exit.

And once again, the move works like a thrax charm.

On a side note, one serious perk of being royal is that we have a private transfer station right inside our palace of Arx Hall. Talk about convenient.

Once Father is far enough behind me, I make a beeline for my private chambers. Along the way, I ask a messenger to request that our royal librarian, Clara, send me everything we have on the Viking Games.

Just thinking about Clara makes me smile. The woman is an exceptional bundle of gray hair and mad skills.

Thrax life is divided into Houses. Clara's father is from my house, Rixa. Her mother hails from the House of Striga. The latter bloodline means that Clara is a rather talented witch. Chances are, she'll have a pile of books waiting in my library before I even reach the room myself.

In my experience, nothing is more important than knowing an excellent librarian.

Arx Hall is a maze of passages. It takes a little while, but I finally reach my private chambers. Like the rest of the palace, my rooms are a medieval-style mixture of tapestries, stone walls, and heavy wooden furniture. I debate about catching some sleep—midnight hunts can take a toll—but I'm curious if Clara has literally worked her magic.

So I head straight for my personal library. Sure enough, there's already a shelf packed with fresh titles about the Norse Universe.

How does she do that, exactly?

To prep for this evening, I spend the rest of my day reading. Of particular interest are the many unique monsters of the Norse Universe. As I do my thing, servants come and go with messages and meals. A few say *happy birthday,* but those words are always accompanied by a pained look. They don't say anything out loud, but I can sense their thoughts easily enough.

You carry too much responsibility for one so young.

There's more to life than duty.

Why don't you ever smile?

These pitying looks have been coming my way for

years. Time was, I'd respond by sharing how Emperor Augustus took power at eighteen. These days, I simply avoid the sad stares and focus on my work instead.

Yes, I'm lonely.

And no, there's nothing to be done about it.

In my world, duty always comes first.

Eventually, it's time to get ready for the Viking Games. Normally, I'd wear the traditional outfit for thrax royalty. By this I mean leather pants, chain mail and a velvet tunic with my house crest of an attacking eagle. But I'm not looking to advertising my noble status tonight. Instead, I plan to blend in with the ghoul population. Since the undead wear dark robes, I choose to wear a black leather duster.

With that, I'm ready for the Viking Games.

5

MYLA

*F*uuuuuuuuuuuuck.

       I stare at the kitchen clock and try not to lose my cool.

Walker and I never do make a fast exit for the Viking Games. Instead, Mom launches into her *greatest hits of anxiety.* Sure, Walker and I could just take off anyway, but that would be hella mean. No way can I leave Mom alone and freaking out while I slip away for some fun.

So my honorary older brother and I listen to Mom's growing list of concerns about moi. It all starts with how I mostly eat from the *sugar food group.* Then Mom segues over to her worries about my lack-o-friends, sassy mouth, and general bad attitude toward our ghoul overlords. At last, she goes off to take a nap.

Halle-freaking-lujah.

With Mom a-snooze, Walker and I finally step into his portal and exit into a section of the Dark Lands called Phantom Forest. This is a pretty nice spot, even if it is in ghoul territory. We follow a path through the trees to reach the arena's main gateway. After Walker hands over our tickets, the two of us hike up to the top tier of the Viking Arena.

What a view.

This place is about twice the size of what we have in Purgatory. The structure is also brand-spanking new, which is a major change for yours truly. The only negative I can see is how the arena floor is covered in purple sand.

Ever try to run or fight in sand? SUH-ucks. I'll take the dirt of Purgatory's Arena any day.

My focus switches to what's happening on all that violent ground. A pre-show is now in full swing, and it comes complete with musicians, clowns and acrobats. And the best part? Huge versions of Norse monsters hover in the sky. It's like a projected float from a human parade. I count a dwarf, some massive snake thing and even some elves. Hella cool.

Walker taps my shoulder, jarring me out of my reverie. "Would you like to take your seat?"

"Oh, yeah. Forgot about that part."

Walker gestures to the end of the very end of a nearby marble bench. "Here you go."

I park my butt. "We didn't miss the battle, right?"

"No, the pre-show goes on for a while. When the actual fight starts, you'll know it." Walker tilts his head. "Do you want some snacks?"

"Yes! Anything with sugar, but especially cotton candy and chocolate. Oh, and hot dogs."

"You got it."

Walker takes off into the shadows. While he's off rounding up some grub, I take a closer look at the audience itself. The arena is packed. I count thrax, ghouls, quasis and even some humans in the mix. The structure also sports two fancy balconies, one on either side. We have the same deal in Purgatory. Back home, one balcony is reserved for Armageddon, the King of Hell, while the other balcony acts as a *home away from home* for Verus, the Queen of the Angels.

Leaning forward, I scan the balcony below me. A big question appears. *Who counts as a muckity-muck in the Dark Lands?* Unfortunately, it's too dark to see anyone. Bummer.

Walker returns with soda, cotton candy, chocolate bars and hot dogs. Delish! I start off with the hot dogs, which are served in shiny tinfoil paper. Once that's in my stomach, I move onto sugary stuff. In no time, I've downed everything and am happily loosening the band on my fancy pants.

With my feast over, I refocus on Walker. My honorary brother keeps staring at that balcony. I know the determined look in his eyes.

I gently elbow Walker and nod toward the spot in question. "Know someone down there?"

"No, never."

It's rare that I can tell Walker is lying. This is one of those times. But before I can tease Walker about it, the lights on the arena dim.

The games are about to begin.

I drop all thoughts of the mystery person on the balcony below me. After all, I can tease Walker later.

A drum beats. The crowd claps in time with the rhythm. This goes on and on until the beats go so fast, the crowd is just clapping and cheering their guts out. Music rises. It's a little plinky-plink for my taste, but then again, Kell is a dark elf. They're known for badass looks and creepy child-like music. The scent of rotting flowers fills the air.

So far, I am not impressed.

In the darkness, a huge figure appears. It's an illuminated version of Ringmaster Kell that appears to stands directly on the arena floor. Like the pre-show Norse monsters, the ringmaster's body is a 3D projection that's both semi-transparent and shiny.

"I am Ringmaster Kell!"

Everyone cheers.

"Welcome to tonight's big match! Two new warriors are here, a father and son who've chosen the stage names of Lash and Shield."

A pair of small figures step out onto the purple sands of the arena. Both wear light body armor and hefty helmets. Some decent applause follows, but it's nothing huge. I'm guessing it takes time to build a following.

Giant Kell pipes up again. "Now Lash and Shield shall speak the vow!"

Although I'm sure the two warriors are screaming their heads off, their voices sound like little squeaks.

We commit our lives to the Viking Games!

As vows go, it's pretty short, which I consider a good thing. In Purgatory, our arena ceremonies can take for-bleeding-ever.

Once the vow part is done, purple sand churns around the warriors' feet. The effect reminds me of two small whirlpools. The ground then climbs up the two guys, surrounding them in a violet shell.

So that's weird.

Just when I'm starting to wonder if Lash and Shield can still breathe, the violet particles tumble off their bodies. Lash and Shield look the same, only each warrior now has a glowing blue mark on their arms, as well as fresh weapons in their hands. For Lash's, both his tattoo and weapon and a whip. The Shield gets a dinky sword-n-shield combo.

My tail pops up over my shoulder. The arrowhead ends wags from side to side. I give it a friendly pat. "I know, boy. When it comes to weapons, you're far more interesting, but nobody in Purgatory cheers for you." I lean in closer. "Yaaaaaay! That's in your honor."

Walker joins in because he's just that amazing. "Yay!"

Giant Kell speaks again. "And now, Lash and Shield shall fight a creature that does not exist in this reality. Feast your eyes on the deadly Norse Fossegrim!"

Giant Kell blinks out of sight. At the same time, the purple sands bubble up into another pile on the arena floor. When the particles rolls down once again, there's now a massive swamp monster standing in the same spot. I'm talking scaly skin, two pokey holes for a nose and claw-like hands.

Oh, yeah. This is getting good.

I pop in a ton of gum. My mouth is so full, I'm having trouble keeping my lips closed as I chew.

And I'm having the best night ever.

6

MYLA

*T*he fun doesn't last long, though.

Here's the deal. I watch pro wrestling matches on the Human Channel (it's not like we have a ton of TV viewing options). And this battle against a so-called Norse monster? It's kinda-sorta the same thing. There are a bunch of coordinated hits and counter strikes.

Color me not-impressed.

Plus, I check the catalog Walker got me from the concession stand. There are no girl warriors here, ever. *What the Hell?*

Plus-PLUS, the catalog openly talks about how Ring-master Kell uses his magic to guide both the warriors fight. No wonder this battle has all the spontaneity of a puppet show.

To kill time, I fold my catalog into origami shapes. Like a headless bird. A lopsided airplane. And a skinny accordion. The fight drags on. Eventually, Lash and the Shield knock out the swamp dude. Woot.

Giant Kell reappears. "I call this match for Lash and Shield!" The crowd goes nutso. More music swells. Giant Kell speaks once more. "Return tomorrow night for another monster match up!"

The music dies down; the image of the ringmaster vanishes. The lights rise.

It's over.

I lean back on my bench while Walker glares at the balcony again. He seems to be focusing on one guy in particular. All I can see is the dude's back, but that's more than enough for me to tease Walker.

Hey, it could be more interesting than that fight.

I elbow my honorary undead brother. "The guy in the leather duster… is he the same one who you were watching before?"

Walker rounds on me. "There is no one in the balcony that you would ever, ever be interested in."

I kick my legs forward. "You know I'm not boy crazy." I tap my chin. "Or do I have secret admirer?"

Walker rises. "This evening is over."

I chuckle. "Walker thinks I have a booooooyfriend. I'm getting maaaaarried."

This is a really immature move, by the way. But in my defense, I'm fifteen. More importantly, it's rare to find a nerve ending in Walker where he freaks out this much. I swear, the guy's entire body is shaking.

"Let's go." Walker grabs my wrist, opens a portal, and pulls me in.

Too funny. What Walker doesn't know is that he has no reason to worry. I have no plans to fall in love, let alone to marry.

Ever.

7

LINCOLN

I set my hip against the waist-high metal barrier that surrounds the balcony.

Tonight's game is over. Lash and Shield won.

Below me, the audience streams up the aisles in their rush to leave. I come to a final conclusion. I'm giving Father a solid *no* on creating a safe zone here for thrax.

My reasons are simple. Sure, warriors and spectators enter the games of their own free will. And it's no secret that Kell commands the moves of his fighters. That's fine for the Viking Games. It's just not the thrax way.

A voice sounds behind me. "What did you think? Would you like to join the games?"

Turning around, I find Ringmaster Kell. "I appreciate the offer, but this isn't for me."

"But when your father invited me on demon patrol, he made it seem you'd all want a refuge here."

"I don't see that happening. This place isn't right for my people, either."

"Why not? Is the fighting not real enough for you? I have to control warriors with my magic because I don't have good raw material to work with. I need better fighters." His features tighten with anger. "I've sacrificed too much for these games to be less than perfect."

My brows lift. "And what did you sacrifice, exactly?"

Moments ago, Kell seemed calm. Now the ringmaster pounds his chest. "I'm the one asking questions here. Doesn't the weight of the crown sit heavily upon you? Wouldn't you like a different future?"

The angrier Kell gets, the easier it is for me to stay calm. "I thought my life was *my father's* to use as he saw it."

Kell stalks closer. "Allow *me* to deal with King Connor. My invitation is for you. No one enters the games without consent. Do you agree to join?"

I eye Kell from head to toe. The ringmaster runs a successful fighting show where he commands every move. Yet it's not enough. *What is this guy's problem?*

I shake my head. *Not sure I want to know.*

"Look," I begin. "I didn't want to join the Viking

Games when you asked me in Brazil. I'm even less interested now."

"So you say. But I've the patience of Odin."

I tilt my head. "Meaning?"

"You're already my warrior. You just don't know it yet."

Smoke billows around Kell. When the green mist vanishes, the ringmaster is gone as well.

BACULUM

Right after the marriage of Lincoln and Myla

LINCOLN

TWENTY YEARS OLD

I've fought twelve demons at once. When a wall of magical fire loomed ahead, I rode my horse through the blaze at full gallop. While fighting a magma monster, I tumbled head-first into a live volcano. In every case, the odds were against me, yet I emerged victoriously.

My warriors call me *fortune's favorite.*

Looking back, all that luck is nothing compared to this moment. I'm a part-angel king who was raised to marry for duty. Finding love was supposed to be impossible. And wedding a part-demon queen? That should have been unthinkable.

But as of yesterday, Myla Lewis became my bride. And this morning, she rests in my bed.

Fortune's favorite indeed.

Myla's waves of red hair fan out behind her on the pillow. The cotton sheet clings to her lovely curves. Even asleep, there's a tension and life to her that shines out across the room. My angelbound love.

I shake my head. *How can this amazing woman want me?* I'm an uptight royal with nothing but obligations to offer her. But somehow, she's here.

What a gift.

With gentle movements, I prop my weight onto my right elbow. Using my free arm, I pull a very-asleep Myla under the covers until her naked curves press against my bare flesh. Warmth radiates wherever we touch. As my bride shifts, a gentle sound emanates from her lips. I lean in for a better listen.

Turns out, my woman has her sleeping quirks. With every inhale, Myla makes a little snort. That's unexpected. How wondrous that I have a lifetime to learn her every secret and eccentricity.

Myla's eyes flutter open. She begins the day with a snarky smile. "Good morning, Mister the King."

Leaning down, I rub my nose along the length of hers. "And the same to you, Madame the Queen."

Here's what that means. Yesterday, Myla and I only planned to get married. But thanks to some drama with the Earl of Acca, we also become King and Queen of Antrum.

That wasn't the sole surprise, either.

Myla's also a supernatural being called the Great Scala, meaning she's the only being who can move souls to Heaven or Hell using tiny supernatural lightning bolts called igni. Last night, those igni announced that Myla was pregnant.

That makes us man and wife.

King and Queen.

Father and mother.

All in one day.

Plus, I finally got to kill Aldred. I consider that part an extra bonus.

Sure, Myla and I had to fight off the King of Hell during our wedding proper. But doesn't everyone have a few things go off the rails during their nuptials?

With gentle movements, I set my palm against her stomach. "Good morning, little Maxon."

Myla frowns. "You don't think it's too soon for a baby?"

In this moment, I know I've been waiting for a child all my life. I brush my thumb in gentle arcs on Myla's belly. "No, it's perfect timing."

"Hey, there. You've been thinking about parenting for a while, haven't you?"

"What makes you say that?"

"Only because you plan everything years in advance. Why would a kid be any different?"

I can't help but smile. Before Myla, I'd been so alone. People wanted things from me, even my parents.

Who am I kidding? Especially my parents.

But with Myla, everything is easy, natural and fun. She isn't asking me about Maxon because she has her own ideas about parenthood and wants to sway my point of view. Myla's genuinely curious. She cares.

"I haven't thought about it formally, but I suppose I have a few ideas."

"Lay it on me."

"To begin with, my parents did a lot of things right. They always had ultimate faith in my skills. Their joy in my achievements was real."

Myla gives me the side eye. "But?"

I tilt my head and think things through. "From a young age, it was clear that I was far more advanced than my peers. My parents didn't want me to be held back by the limitations of others. They had me raised, trained and tutored solo."

Myla scrunches up her features in disgust. "That sucks. I didn't like my peers, except for Cissy. But at least I knew them. What else?"

"I was born with a massive *to do list*. I want our son to have some freedom."

"Ooh, that's a good idea." Myla rests her hand atop mine. I grin. This is the first time we've both touched her stomach in honor of Maxon. My heart warms.

"What about you?" I ask. "I'm certain you have some plans as well."

Myla winks. "You know me. I'm with you on the responsibilities thing. My first arena death match took place when I was way too young." Myla's tail pops up from the covers. The arrowhead-shaped end moves up and down in a way that says, *oh yes.*

Myla continues. "Plus, my mother was hella over-protective. Although, she had her reasons, considering how my secret father was actually an archangel. Still, I always knew Mom worried about me because she cared. Octavia is like that, too."

The words hang out there, if unsaid. *But it's not that way with Connor.*

I roll onto my back and stare up at the ceiling. "My father has his reasons, too."

Myla curls up against my side. "Want my take on Connor?"

"I'd love it."

"This is going to start with Cissy, but it will circle around. You with me?"

"Always."

"Well, Cissy's mother constantly bitches about how

hard it was to be pregnant. Cis has a golden retriever's tail and I guess it was wagging all the time. Whatever. Then, when the actual birth happened, it lasted for days because Cissy has a super-large head."

I purse my lips and think this through. "Now that you say it, she does have a plus-sized noggin."

"It's why she styles her hair into Shirley Temple curls. She thinks it hides her massive face. Anyway, Cissy's mom was always saying how this terrible pregnancy meant that Cis has to do *fill in the blank*. Like one time, Cis had to hang up some old ugly painting in her room just because her dad stole it." Myla clears her throat. "Excuse me. Cissy wants me to say that her father reappropriates stuff."

"What was the painting?" We're going off the rails here, but I can't help it. As thievery goes, Cissy's father has excellent taste.

"The painting showed some old couple dressed in black with wacky neck gear. The artist was..." Myla snaps her fingers. "I've got it. Remmy-somebody."

"Was the painting *A Lady And Gentleman In Black* by Rembrandt?"

"Yes. How'd you know?"

"It was taken as part of a famous heist on Earth. Please continue."

"Anyway, the way Connor acts, he reminds me of

Cissy's mother. It's like your father made some great sacrifice to bring you into this world, and now you owe him forever."

For a long minute, I stare at the ceiling and consider Myla's words. "You have a point. Connor carries a sense of…" I tilt my head, trying to find the right word.

"Entitlement?"

"Yes. That." Emotions battle it out inside me. First, there's the joy of revelation. *One mystery about Connor is solved!* That's quickly followed by a spike of anger. I know Father has his reasons, but that doesn't make his actions right.

A series of heavy knocks sound at the door. My reception room is only accessible by a long hallway, so whoever's visiting must be slamming with full force. Myla and I both freeze.

"It can't be," she whispers.

Sure enough, a familiar voice echoes down through the hall. "Good morning, son!"

I pull Myla against me. "We can ignore him, you know."

She rolls her eyes. "I don't know. He's a persistent guy."

"True." An idea appears. "There's a special palace for royal honeymoons. Tradition dictates no one can disturb us there."

Myla raises her hand. "Count me in."

"We'll move there tonight."

Heavy knocks sound again. "Lincoln, my boy! I know you can hear me!"

Guilt weighs onto my shoulders. "Sorry about this. Once I answer the door, Father will want to talk."

"You want company?"

"No. If you're with me, then I can't use you as an excuse to leave."

"Damn, you are so sneaky, it's awesome." Myla stretches. "Take all the time you need. I have to shower anyway." A sly look shines in her eyes.

Which means one thing. Chances are, Myla's totally going to check out my bathroom. Fortunately, I have something special planned for the occasion.

"Have fun," I say. Then I pull on some jeans and go to face Father.

2

MYLA

NINETEEN

ho asks for a father-son talk on the first day of their kid's honeymoon?

Connor, that's who.

While Lincoln and his dicky dad chat away, I sashay into the bathroom. With every step, my tail swipes angrily behind me. After I slam the door, I realize the truth.

I'm focusing on the wrong thing here. Who cares about Connor when it's bathroom snooping time? After all, it's like the universe is saying... *Myla, check out Lincoln's secret guy stuff.*

Who am I to deny fate?

Ever since I met Lincoln, his home in Antrum has always held a magnetic interest. Some key questions.

What do thrax do for entertainment without television?

How do they manage getting clean without commercially-developed body products?

Are their medicine cabinets stocked with aspirin, magical leeches or what?

Now, I'll finally get some answers.

First things first. I check the shower. It's a large tiled space with lots of enchanted nozzles that spray water in every direction. A little shelf holds a single bar of piney-smelling soap. I double check, just to make sure I didn't miss anything.

A little disappointing in its meh-ness.

Moving on to the medicine cabinet.

At least, I assume it's the medicine cabinet. Thrax are all stuck in the middle ages, so Lincoln's wall holds a pair of gilded mirrors that sit above matching porcelain sinks. And between those mirrors? Another pair of tiny doors are set directly into the wall itself.

That says *medicine cabinet* to me.

Oh, the things I might discover. What kind of magical goop do thrax use when they get ready? I'm really pulling for some live leeches in jars. Or perhaps a few slugs in a petri dish. It's just the romantic in me.

I pull open the side door to find teensy shelves lined with small clay jars. The labels are boring stuff like aspirin and shaving cream.

No slugs or leeches. Oh, well.

Opening the right-hand door, I find a fresh tube of regular human-style toothpaste and some dental floss. There are even untouched brushes, both of the tooth and hair variety. Maybe my pregnancy hormones are kicking in, but that's about the cutest thing I've ever seen.

Lincoln went out and got me morning stuff. *Sniff, sniff!*

Once I'm showered, I open the bathroom door a crack again. No Lincoln. My guy must be in his reception room with Connor. I tilt my head and listen closely. They're in the reception, all right. I can't catch what they're saying, but the tones are distinctly angry.

Better get dressed and join in the fun. Because when Connor is involved, there's always some drama.

3

LINCOLN

or the last hour, Father and I have stood in my reception chamber. It's a large room with leather couches and heavy tapestries. Right now, it only lacks one thing.

The truth.

Father keeps stalling around. Even he wouldn't interrupt my honeymoon without a serious purpose. It's all frustrating in the extreme.

Myla steps into the room. She wears a loose tunic dress and a frown. *How perfect.* "What's going on, Connor?"

Father folds his arms over his chest. "I can't talk with *her* here."

The way Father says *her,* the word drips with disdain. My last thread of patience snaps.

"Enough! You barge in here and refuse to give any details. Now you insult my wife by insinuating she has no right to know why her own honeymoon is being disrupted. I'll give you one last chance. Why are you here?"

Father's shoulders slump. "I know about the baby."

Myla and I exchange a look. She angles her head in a way that says, *how do you want to work this?*

I give her the barest shake of my head. *Say nothing.*

We both move to face Connor once more. Long seconds tick by while both of us glare at my father. This is a trick I've learned over the years, by the way. People hate a silent stare, especially if it's two against one.

Sure enough, Father cracks. "You're probably wondering how I know about the baby."

"Go on," I state.

"It was Myla's igni," says Father. "They appeared to me and your mother." He gestures toward Myla. "Your parents were told as well. The igni even gave us the baby's name."

Myla is a supernatural being called the Great Scala. Igni are her little lightning bolts of power. It's not surprising that igni would have appeared to our parents last night. They certainly showed up to me and Myla to announce the pregnancy.

Myla closes her eyes. A serene look settles on her

face, followed by a wince. I've seen this before. Myla can reach out to her igni through her mind. When she winces, it means that she's chatting away with her invisible minions.

"Everything all right?" I ask.

Myla opens her eyes. "Fine. My igni confirmed everything. They totally blabbed to both our parents."

Father smiles, but there's no real joy in the expression. "Right after I found out, I went to the Dark Lands and spoke to Ringmaster Kell."

"We talked about this years ago," I state. "Kell and the Viking Games are not suitable for, well, anything. Why would you see the ringmaster?

"Because of Armageddon." All the color drains from father's face. "The King of Hell tried to break into your wedding. You aren't safe. Little Maxon is at risk, too!"

When I next speak, I force my tone to stay even. "I understand that there's been a lot of change in the last few days. Myla and I are now King and Queen. Armageddon tried to break into our wedding. And we are expecting a baby. It's a lot for anyone to handle. I can understand why you'd want to run off and help, but I don't see how Ringmaster Kell can affect things, one way or another."

An almost manic gleam shines in father's eyes. "The ground of the Viking Games actually comes from another reality. It's not subject to our laws. Even Armageddon cannot break through the purple sands of the Viking Arena."

Father is being a little hyper, but I've seen proven warriors break down over far less. And it is true that the Viking Arena is impermeable to Armageddon, assuming Ringmaster Kell casts some magical wards of blocking.

"What are you thinking?" asks Myla. "Do you suggest we bring some of that purple sand down to Antrum?"

"That could work," I state. "There are rumors someone already brought purple sand into Antrum. If I remember right, it's deep under Gurith territory and is used to protect some storage area."

Father raises his hands, palms forward. "No, I'm not suggesting anything like that. Here's what I love done for you. Kell has agreed to build a dwelling for your family directly underneath his arena. You can live there in safety."

Myla and I exchange a blank look. We're constantly getting offered odd things, even houses.

"That's…" Myla smacks her lips, trying to find the right words. "Something."

I force a smile. "This was kind of you, but we can't possibly—" I'm about to say *live there* when Father jumps in.

"I knew you'd be pleased," he interrupts. A genuine

grin brightens his face. "Kell only asks a small price in exchange for keeping you all safe. All he wants is for Maxon to fight in the Viking Games starting at age sixteen."

"Let me get this straight," I clarify. "Kell wants Maxon to vow he'll never leave the Viking Arena."

"Of course." Father looks genuinely stunned. I can't tell if he's deluding himself or just putting on an exceptionally good show today. "What's wrong with that?"

"Read my lips," says Myla. "*No, no and no.* Our family will never move into the Viking Arena. Lincoln and I understand that you're freaking out, but you need to drop this whole thing."

Father takes a half-step backward. Tears well in his eyes. "I'm just keeping my grandson safe."

"No one questions your goals here," I state. "But decisions about Maxon's life are for me and Myla alone."

Father's demeanor instantly changes. All signs of sorrow vanish as his eyes flash with anger. "I may no longer be king, but I am still the eldest man in this family. In the Norse Universe, I have rights. My grandson *will* be raised on Kell's property. Maxon shall train to become a great warrior in the Viking Games."

Father's words pierce my heart like an arrow. I hear them echo in my mind, over and over.

In the Norse Universe, I have rights.

"Father," I say, my voice hoarse. "What did you do?"

"Maxon is my grandson, and I'm going to do what I think is best for his future." Connor reaches into his pocket and pulls out a round rock covered in small markings. "This runestone represents my unbreakable oath to Kell. The ringmaster and I formed a blood covenant last night. No matter where you may hide, my grandson will be magically transported to his new home just after birth."

Pain and sorrow radiate through my rib cage. "What?"

Father lifts his chin. "I have the right to cast this spell and make this vow. This is a matter of the Norse Universe, not Antrum. You cannot stop this thing from happening."

All my previous emotions melt into rage. I stalk closer to Father. "From the moment I was born, you had work for me to do. I was kept isolated, alone, and tied to my duty. Now you want to do the same thing to my son?" I swipe the stone from his hand. "This is not a spell. It's a symbol of you trying to rule Maxon's life, just as you did mine. And this vow will be crushed, mark my words."

"That's impossible." Father turns to Myla. "You can't agree with this."

Myla chuckles. "Oh, I agree all right." Her eyes flash red with fury. "Every spell has a breaking point. Lincoln and I will find it."

Father refocuses on me. "Be reasonable. You'd can't murder the ringmaster just to end this spell."

"There's no need to kill anyone," I explain. "I'm sure the Ringmaster can be reasoned with." I tighten my grip on the stone. "And when that happens, this stone will turn to dust."

Father shakes with rage. "I won't allow it. You can't end my plans."

"And *you* can't make decisions for my family." I cross the room and open the door. "Excuse us. You've done enough for one day."

Father stalks out without saying another word. It takes everything in me not slam the door behind him. Once Father is well and gone, I turn to Myla.

"Looks like we have work to do."

4

MYLA

W hat a shit show.

Lincoln smirks. "How does this rank on the Myla meter?"

In reply, I give my classic *meter arm move*. This involves setting my left forearm parallel with the floor while making my right forearm point to the ceiling.

"Meter says…" I angle my right forearm so it points toward the side wall. Then I shimmy my arm more furiously. "And—BLAM!—the meter blows up. Officially, this is a disaster."

Many folks would have no clue what I'm doing right now. Lincoln not only gets me, he chuckles. Dimples are involved. Total marital bonus.

Lincoln shakes his head. "Only you could make me smile right now."

"Everything's an adventure if you have the right attitude."

"And the right partner."

Yes, our honeymoon just got torpedoed and yet, we're rolling with it. *Marrying Lincoln? Best decision ever.*

A question appears. "Hey, why wasn't Octavia here?"

Lincoln taps his chin. "Father must not have told her about it. If he had…" Lincoln lets the thought sit out there.

"He'd be icing his balls right now," I finish.

Which isn't too crazy. The first time Connor and Octavia met, she took him down with a knee to the crotch.

Lincoln taps his cheek. "Do you think Father told your parents about his plan with Kell? They must have spoken, considering how Connor knew where your igni gave them the news about Maxon."

I scrunch my mouth onto one side of my face and consider things. "Our parents probably all chatted about the baby. That's it. They wouldn't want to bug us on our honeymoon. You know, except Connor."

Lincoln sighs. "Should we tell them what Father did?"

"No. Fucking. Way."

Lincoln chuckles. "No, what you *really* think?"

"Hey, my father is general of the archangels. If he

believes his grandchild is at risk, my dad will summon his entire angelic army like that." I snap my fingers. "And let's not forget my Mom. She's the President of Purgatory. At a minimum, her special forces will get called in. Then there will be a massive attack on both the Purple Salient and the Viking Games. We're talking inter-realm war."

"That's true." Lincoln rubs his neck for a minute. "And Octavia would do her bit as well. Half the after-realms owes my mother a favor. I hate to think who she'd bring into the mix."

"Plus, once all our parents know, then the entire after-realms will learn about this *fuckfest du Connor*. Think about it. My people freak out if I have a bad hair day. Can you imagine what would happen if they thought I was being sent to live on ghoul territory?"

"You're right. We need to keep this quiet." Lincoln turns the stone over in his hands and scans the runes. "This says that Kell is magically bound to house us and will never allow Armageddon onto his property." He flips the pendant over and reads more runes. "And in return, Maxon will fight in the Warrior Games forever."

I try to find a bright side. It isn't easy. "At least, the runestone backs up what Connor said about the vow to Kell."

The muscles in Lincoln's jawline tense up. "I never

trusted that ringmaster. Kell must think us weak indeed to agree something like this. This runestone represents nothing less than a threat from the ringmaster to both you and Maxon."

Lincoln rarely works himself up into a rage, but when it happens? Watch out.

I cross the room to stand directly before my husband. Before I speak, I take care to meet his gaze straight on. "Look, there must be some way to break Connor's magical vow. Sure, Kell is a douchebag. But maybe we don't have to deal with him at all. Let's focus on ways to smash that spell and get on with our honeymoon."

Lincoln takes in a slow breath. "My library holds many books on the Viking Games. Perhaps something in there can help."

My guy offers his hand and I take it. Side by side, we walk off toward what I hope will be just another adventure.

5

LINCOLN

Myla and I scour my library. Hours fly by. We find quite a few books on the Norse Universe, the best of which get piled onto my main table. As we work, my temper cools. The more I think about it, it's obvious that we'll find a solution.

Over time, my thoughts circle back to our honeymoon. Once this runestone is destroyed, then Myla and I can get back to enjoying our time together.

It's a reflex to keep brushing Myla's thighs and arms while we work. Myla is a quasi-demon. All her people have a tail as well as a power across the seven deadly sins. In Myla's case, her abilities span wrath—which makes her a great warrior—and lust—which means that she definitely notices all my extra touches.

As a matter of fact, when Myla's lust powers are activated, her irises glow red. I call it sparking. And indeed, Myla sparks quite a few times during our research.

What can I say? A man needs a hobby.

Right now, I sit on a high-back chair before the main table. Myla sits on the tabletop itself. A heavy leather book rests on her lap.

Myla taps the page. "I've got something. Underland."

"Excellent." I rest my palms on Myla's knees. Little by little, I slide Myla's body toward me. I stop once we're facing each other.

Myla fights a grin. "What are you up to?"

I brush my thumbs against the inside of her knees. "Do you have any idea how many nights I sat in this library and dreamed about you? And now, you're here as my wife."

She blushes. "Focus, Lincoln."

"I am. You were saying something about underwear." I slide my hands up her thighs. "And you're wearing a thong. Naughty girl."

"Do you mind?" She holds up her book. "I have very important research here."

"I'm listening. I'm just multi-tasking."

When Myla next speaks, her voice is low and husky. "I know my eyes have been sparking."

"It's one of my favorite looks on you. Keep talking." I

massage her thighs in a slow rhythm. "You were saying. Underland."

Myla shoots me a frown, but there's no real anger in the expression. "Back with Connor, you talked a place under Gurith territory in Antrum."

"It's a storage area." I alternate between deep massage and light touches. "It's supposed to be protected by the purple sands of the Viking Arena."

"Well, this book calls it Underland," says Myla. "There are instructions about how to get there by Pulpitum and… mmmmmm. You're totally distracting me."

"No, I'm not. You were clearly saying something about Underland." I move to massage deep between her thighs.

"Fuck research time. You've already memorized everything in this library, right?"

"Not that book. Keep going."

"But you're really really reeeeeeeeally distracting."

I freeze my hands in place. "Does that mean you're giving into my manly skills?"

"What a meanie you are. You know I can't resist a challenge."

I press my fingertips harder between her thighs. "So keep going. What else does it say?"

"There's supposed to be, um, a tree in Underland that

has golden apples. If you pick one of the apples you get a wish. This is magic comes from the same world as the Viking Games, so we can use it to…"

I stop once again. *Yes, I am a mean meanie.*

"Lincoln."

"What?"

"You stopped."

"Well, you reached a really good part of the story."

When Myla next speaks, her speech comes out so quickly, it sounds like one long word. "Destroythatrunestone." She tosses the book over her shoulder. It's a move that says, *research time is over.*

I lock gaze with hers. "So we'll go to Underland, get the apple, and fix everything. Well done. We might even destroy this runestone within twenty-four hours—and all without bothering to see Kell."

"Yes." She links her legs around my torso and pulls me closer. "I'm just that awesome."

In reply, I yank off my T-shirt. Myla runs her hands across my bare chest. Everywhere we touches, my skin heats with desire. Within seconds, both of us naked. Myla stays seated on the table. I stand.

And we enjoy each other fully.

Afterward, Myla and I spend hours finding new ways to fin the same joy in other parts of the chamber. One thing I'll say about this honeymoon. I'll never look at my library the same way again.

6

MYLA

*S*o this is fun.

Lincoln and I enjoy what I call the Three S-es, namely Sex, Shower, and Snacks. In our case, the shower stuff also includes more sex, so that's an extra bonus.

Afterward, Lincoln and I hit the demon patrol gear room and get tricked out for our trip to Lower Gurith. By the time we're done, Lincoln wears his black body armor while I sport my favorite dragonscale fighting suit. Both of us also drag along backpacks stuffed with awesome camping stuff.

It's all part of our cover story that we're taking a break from the palace to go on a camping trip in Lower Gurith. Word's already gotten around that Connor stopped by and bothered us. No one questions why we'd want to rough it out in some empty caves.

This is my first time camping, and I'm not too excited about the idea. Never gone before and certainly haven't had the desire. Not that many folks hang out in the wilds of Purgatory. There's way too much rain. In my opinion, if the Almighty wanted us to camp, then he wouldn't have invented five-star hotels.

With our fake gear in hand, Lincoln and I take the Pulpitum to Lower Gurith. When the platform comes to a stop, we step out into a massive cavern that's made of rough stone. it's not like I expected to walk out off the platform and just see a tree sitting here.

But yeah. Maybe I thought that might happen a little bit.

Fine. This won't be easy. Time to call in the big guns. Closing my eyes, I call out to my igni with my mind.

Need your help, little ones.

In reply, my head fills with what sounds like the world's worst case of speaker feedback. Wincing, I cover my ears. I'm not giving up, though.

I need to find the golden apple tree of the goddess Idunn. Where is it?

The mechanical screeching just gets louder. I do catch some words in there though.

Maxon... fear... no apple... no help.

Sometimes, my igni can be awesome. In other instances, they suck. Like now, for example. I straighten my spine and keep going. This is for my son.

Come on, you little lighting bolts of annoyance. You can't just refuse to help. Where's the tree already?

The feedback loop gets louder than ever. Their little voices rise to a howl.

We gooooo!

All the noise disappears from my mind. I'd call them again, but I know there's no point. When it comes to magical help, I have the divas of the supernatural world. Asking them again will only mean it takes longer for them to reply.

What a bunch of little bitches.

LOWER GURITH

7

LINCOLN

*H*aving grown up in Antrum, I can read caves easily. Turns out, this particular cavern has a rather interesting tale to share.

"What do you see?" asks Myla.

"These tracks here." I gesture to a line of markings on the floor. "Hundreds of people walked through this place. A few adults. Many children."

"Children? How young?"

"Five, maybe six years old. Based on the state of the tracks, I'd say that no one's been through this spot in a thousand years."

"Let me get this straight," says Myla. "A thousand years ago, a bunch of kids walked into this place and never left." She scans the room. "That's wild. Do you think it's some kind of deception spell?"

"No." Kneeling, I touch the cave floor once. Sure enough, faint vibrations move up my arms. "They're still here."

"No. Way." Myla steps around in a slow circle, as if seeing the place for the first time. "It just looks like a regular old cave."

"It isn't. I sense magic. There's a ward spell here or something. It's supposed to…" I frown, trying to find the right words.

"Drive us away," finishes Myla. "I got the same vibe. It says *get out now*. My guess? Someone's hiding in here. Maybe more than one person. And they've got themselves an apple tree."

"Agreed."

Myla cups her hand by her mouth. "Hey guys! I'm Queen Myla and this is King Lincoln. We're here to get a golden apple to save our son. Long story. Anyway, will you help us?"

Silence.

Myla smacks her lips. "Well, it was worth a try." She rounds on me. "Any ideas where we can find that tree? If a bunch of kids want to attack us along the way, I'll guess we'll just wing it." Myla's tail swoops from side to side in a movement that says, *just try to attack us.*

I turn the runestone over in my hands. "As a matter

of fact, I think this rock can help. The markings shine more brightly when I hold it in this direction."

Myla grins. "Oh, like a compass."

"Precisely." I hoist my backpack on my shoulders and turn to Myla. "I can carry yours as well, if you like."

"No, thanks. I'm not *that* pregnant yet."

Suddenly, a breeze strikes up out of nowhere. *That's not natural.*

Myla gives me the side eye. "Did you notice that?"

"I did."

Myla cups her hand by her mouth. "Pregnant."

The wind strikes up again. This time, there's the faintest hint of purple light within the mix.

"Oooooooo0okay, then." Myla purses her lips. "So that's strange. I'll just stop saying the p-word for now." She pulls on her own backpack.

"Probably for the best."

And together, we take off for the shadows in the Western side of the cavern.

8

LINCOLN

The hours slog by as Myla and I march through Lower Gurith. The place pulls on my senses in odd ways. Back in Rixa, I can always catch the low murmur of voices, if I really listen. There the air perpetually carries the faint smell of charcoal from the Incaenda, a nearby river that flows with magma. To me, Antrum is both underground and alive, all at once.

That's not how things are here in Lower Gurith.

It's a reflex to keep reaching out with my senses, trying to catch any familiar sounds and smells. There's nothing to detect and that's short circuiting my brain. I can't hear anyone nearby, yet I feel invisible eyes upon us constantly.

Fortunately, the magic that powers all of Antrum stays active even as we step farther into Lower Gurith.

The air stays stale but breathable. Ethereal light reflects the time of the day on the Earth's surface miles above our heads.

Still, as night falls, the sense of danger grows.

Eventually Myla and I decide to make camp. When it comes to packing up, we thrax always save space by using enchanted camping supplies. Most gear gets camouflaged to look like food. A tin of jam turns into a sleeping bag. Cans of olives transform into campfires. A rice box becomes a tent. You get the idea.

It takes some doing, but I convince Myla to eat a meal of something that isn't Demon Bars. That said, I don't have a culinary death wish. When Myla insists that Demon Bars make the perfect dessert after stew, I quickly agree. Then, because I am a natural schemer, I make another request.

At this point, we're sitting on our sleeping bags in front of an enchanted fire. I hold my palm out. "I should very much like some dessert as well."

"Sure." Myla twists to fish through her backpack and grab me a Demon Bar. She pauses. "You know what I found the other day?"

"I can't imagine."

"Some squished-up Demon Bars in your desk drawer."

There's no question where Myla is going with this.

When she and I are out on patrol together, I often "request" a Demon Bar. And I have yet to actually eat one.

I shoot her a sly look. "In my defense, I never actually speak the words, *I will eat a Demon Bar.*"

"You sneak!" Myla gasps. "I see it all now. You just said, and I quote, *I should very much like some dessert.*"

Myla speaks that last sentence while imitating me to perfection. Her impression involves lowering her voice and taking on a certain air of detached badassery.

In reply, I simply lay back on the sleeping bag. I've changed into light armor for sleeping; Myla stays in her dragonscale fighting suit. There's no way we're lounging around in pajamas when *who knows what* is roaming around these caves. Besides, we've packed tons of cleanliness charms. Naturally, they're camouflaged as hand wipes.

"Is that all you're going to say?" asks Myla. "Nothing?"

"It was my plan." I lace my fingers behind my head. "You already know my position on your diet. All is fair in love and making your woman eat something other than sugar."

Normally, Myla would counter by pointing out how she's a demon and can eat anything without gaining an ounce. This time, she rubs her stomach and grins.

"You've got a free pass on the diet stuff for as long as I'm pregnant."

I grin. "Good to know."

Myla lies down and cuddles against my side. "I can't shake the feeling that we're not wanted here."

"It's that warding spell. As we go deeper into the caves, it gets stronger."

"Whoever cast this, they're dreaming if they think some rinky-dink ward will stop us."

I chuckle. "True that."

"When we don't turn back, do you think they'll attack us next?"

I narrow my eyes and consider. "No. If they were going to be aggressive, they would have done it the moment we stepped off the Pulpitum. My guess is there's some kind of barrier up ahead. Whoever hides in this cave will hold that line."

Myla nods. "Enough talk about battle stuff. Tell me about your trip to the Viking Games."

"I only attended once. It's not that great of a story, at least from a fighting point of view. Although, Ringmaster Kell is involved."

"Did you piss him off?"

"Absolutely."

Myla chuckles. "In that case, I can't wait to hear everything."

"The fight involved a swamp monster. It wasn't much of a match. Kell puppeteered the whole thing with his magic."

Myla punches my rib cage. "No way."

"Ouch."

"Sha. You're in body armor. Besides, there are more important things here. As in, I went to that very game with Walker. The swamp thing fought two warriors called the Lash and Shield, am I right?"

"Yes." I shake my head in disbelief. "That's the one."

"Whoa. I can't believe we ended up at the same game."

I sort through my memories of that night. "I viewed everything from a balcony. As I recall, I got the distinct feeling that someone was watching me. Still, I figured it was just an effect of the crowd."

Myla punches me again. "We were sitting in the nosebleeds. Walker kept glaring at the balcony below us. He was totally looking at you. By the way, that leather duster you had on was badass."

"Thank you."

"Wow. I teased Walker crap about staring. Then he rushed us out of the arena."

"Clearly, he was terrified that my sixteen-year-old mojo would prove irresistible."

"Well, Walker might have had a point." She looks up

at me and winks. "All I saw was your back and still I got mightily intrigued."

I shake my head. "What a shame that Walker always took your mother's request to keep you isolated so very seriously. Now years have gone by and he still hasn't said a thing. That's what you call classic Walker."

Long minutes tick by. The darkness seems to press in around even more closely. Myla is first to break the silence. When she speaks, her voice is so low, I can barely make out her words.

"We have to find that golden apple. I lived most of my life as a slave to ghoul overlords. I won't let that happen to our son."

Myla is so brave. Hearing the pain in her voice just about undoes me. I pull her closer against my side. "We won't let that happen. Maxon will have choices." I gently brush my fingers through Myla's hair. "I'll take first watch. You get some rest."

And within minutes, Myla is letting out little snorting as she sleeps.

9

MYLA

The next morning, Lincoln and I wake up, put out the fake fire, and eat some breakfast. It's more canned stew. Bleugh. The stuff is crazy-bland, but eating it makes Lincoln unreasonably happy, so I choke it down.

All in all, the camping side of things is going fine. It's the silent-but-malicious vibe in the air that makes me jumpy.

Still, Lincoln and I actively ignore the hidden watchers as we pack up and follow our little runestone compass deeper into the caves.

Now, most of Antrum is pretty smooth. When Lincoln and I were marching around yesterday, the ground was a little uneven in a few places. Nothing too bad, though.

Today, it's a total nightmare.

About half the time, we either have to crawl on all fours or scale up sheer walls.

After six hours of this, I'm a sweaty mess. And my dragonscale fighting suit is built for short battles, not long hikes. After today and yesterday, I'm now familiar with a new kind of pain.

Thigh chafe. Grrr.

In the end, the runestone tells us to walk through a super thin crack in the wall.

I start missing the time when thigh chafe was my biggest issue. Now I must enter the new and frighting world of severe claustrophobia.

It feels like forever ekes by as we shove ourselves through the skinniest freaking passage in the history of ever. I try to breathe through my nose so I don't hyperventilate. That doesn't help too much. What does work is closing my eyes and imagining my happy place.

Which is Lincoln's library. What can I say? I'm part lust demon. The wheels of my mind tend to spin in certain directions.

At last, we press past the nasty passage and into a larger space.

And what a place it is.

The bland caves we've been marching through are now gone. Instead, our surroundings are replaced by a forest that's unlike anything I've seen on Earth or the after-realms.

I blink hard, not believing what I'm seeing. "We must have reached Underland."

"Indeed."

I lean against Lincoln's side. He wraps his arm around my waist. For a long minute, it's all we can to take in the sight before us.

I've seen fake forests inside the caves of Antrum. What those people can do with gemstones is just amazing. Every once in a while, I've run across a thrax who's pumped in enough magic to grow a tree or two underground.

But this is totally different.

Gray trees reach up into a misty sky. Thin branches drip with purple leaves. Oversized mushrooms dot the scene. The ground is a sheet of grey cobblestones held together with purple mortar.

No, it's purple sand.

And for some reason, just staring at it makes me sick to my stomach.

Hells bells.

UNDERLAND

10

LINCOLN

The analytical side of my brain kicks into high gear, cataloging every purple leaf and oversized mushroom in this place. It's no illusion. There really is a supernatural forest hidden inside my realm, and it comes from another reality.

Sadly, that heavy sense of menace still hangs in the air as well. Something in here hates me and Myla.

It takes an effort of will, by I unwind my arm from around Myla. Side by side, we follow the cobblestone path.

My thoughts spin through all the monsters of the Norse Universe. Could there be a giant snake lurking at the end of this trail? Or perhaps a battle dwarf? We're exploring another slice of reality. Anything is possible.

Myla's gait turns wobbly. Some of the color drains

from her face. I link my fingers with hers. "What's wrong?"

"It started when we crossed into Underland. This purple sand makes my stomach churn. And I shouldn't even be having morning sickness because I've only been pregnant for two days."

"Do you need a healing charm?"

Myla goes on as if I didn't ask a question. She's on a roll. "But I'm a supernatural being and so is our baby. All that magical mojo is mixing with this *very special forest* and making me totally barfy. I could also be feeling extra emotional right now." She sniffles. "It's not fair. I'm built to kill things, not lose my marbles over some freaking sand."

It's healthy for wrath demons to tirade every so often. When I next speak, I take care to use my most comforting voice. "Is there anything else you want to add?"

"No."

"Do you want a healing charm?"

"No again."

I brush a gentle kiss over her cheek. "I love you, my ferocious queen."

Myla lifts her chin. "This is a kind of battle, isn't it?"

"Yes, and you're exceedingly brave."

"Thank you."

A low voice reverberates through the cavern. "Unnnnnhhh."

Both of us freeze. "Did you say that?" I ask.

"Nope," says Myla. And she pops the *p* at the end for extra emphasis.

"Unnnnhhhh!"

Instantly, the two of us go into fighting mode. Myla's tail arches over her shoulder. I pull my baculum from their holster. We walk off into the mist and follow the sound.

What we find is a small wooden building built in the style of a classic thrax outpost. Purple sand covers the cobblestones that lead up to the entrance.

The scene is picture perfect, and yet the sense of doom presses in more fiercely than ever before. From the moment since we entered this realm, something has wanted us to run away in fear.

And now, I'm certain of one thing. That mystery force is right before us.

OUTPOST

11

MYLA

*L*incoln and I wait at the foot of a small hill that's topped by a thrax outpost.

Suddenly, the sky darkens. A spot on the ground bubbles and heaves as someone reaches up from beneath the earth. Their claw-like hand breaks through while clasping a handful of green grass and purple sand. Seconds later, an entire man hauls himself up from the ground.

The dude is totally dead.

I'm talking torn skin, exposed muscles, one ear falling off... the whole deal. At some point, the guy probably wore a tunic and loose pants. Now his outfit is just rags.

Another body rises up to stand beside the first. This one's a woman. She wears a shabby peasant dress and carries a broken basket.

Oooookay. Did not expect that.

Within seconds, a long line of undead have scaled their way out of the earth. It's a group of incredibly dead men and women. Hard to be sure, but it looks like most passed away in their twenties. Now they all stand side by side with military precision.

I notice that one dead dude holds a runestone like ours, only his is much bigger and the markings don't glow. *Huh.* Kell must have transported these folks here from the Nordic Universe. Based on the rags they all wear, it looks like the ringmaster brought over a whole village. Or at least its graveyard.

Not sure I want to know the story behind that one.

"These creatures are what's been giving off that sense of menace," whispers Lincoln. "They're draugar."

The moment he says the word, I remember it from our reading. Draugar are Nordic zombies. I've never killed anything like that before. Is it terrible how I want them to attack? Nah.

The first Draugar steps forward. "Cross line. We kill."

Don't say it.

Don't say it.

Do NOT say it.

Fuck it. I'm saying it.

"Him Lincoln. Me Myla. You dead." All of which is

true. And—perhaps fortunately for me—the Draugar misses my Tarzan-style sarcasm. Lincoln gets it, though. He tries to hide his smirk, but I totally catch it.

And making my guy grin during a zombie encounter? I consider that a big win.

"No cross line! No go to temple!"

Lincoln and I exchange a look. "Oh, we are so going to that temple," I declare.

"Noooooo goooooo to teeeeeeemple!" The Draugar picks up a handful of violet sand and chucks it right in my face.

Big mistake.

DRAUGAR

12

MYLA

*E*ver since we reached Underland, I've been a hot mess in the emotional regulation department.

It's all the fault of my pregnancy and this stupid purple sand.

And that vile stuff got chucked in my mouth. Even on my best days, I'm not Captain Calm. It doesn't go with my *wrath demon situation.*

But right now? I lose my freaking mind.

I march right up to the first Draugar zombie. "You." I poke him in his chest and maybe my finger goes between his ribs a little. I don't even care. "Chuck sand at me again, and you'll lose the rest of your tongue. You hear me, Eddie Eloquence?"

"Unnnnhhh," says the first Draugar. He then moves

to stand behind me.

"Kill you," says the basket lady Draugar. "Kill!" To emphasize her point, she pulls out a butcher knife.

Some small part of me knows that I'm being irrational here. These are unknown monsters from another reality who are threatening me with death. But it turns out that pregnancy hormones are a bitch. I am not putting up with any of this crap.

I round on the Draugar chick next. "Look, Undead Betty Crocker. Back. The Fuck. Off."

She gets behind me, too.

"Line them up and lead them into the outpost," says Lincoln. "I've got some dungeon charms to lock them inside."

I scan the long line of Draugar. They don't look too scary, but there certainly are a lot of them. It would be a major time suck to invest all the hours needed to kill every last one. Also, they really aren't attacking, so there's that. Also-also, they smell like bad breath and dumpster juice. It's making me nauseous again.

Into the outpost they go!

I approach the next Draugar. "You're next, Chinless Wonder." He limps to get behind Undead Betty Crocker. It works so well, I just walk down the line and call out names as I go.

"Start moving, Single Boob Babe. You're next, Mister

No-Pants No-Balls. Pick up the pace, Sir Hopsalot. Just because you have one leg doesn't mean you can't hustle."

All the while, Lincoln fishes through his pack and tries out different charms. None of them work. I blame the purple sand because Hell knows that stuff is screwing with *my* equilibrium.

After about fifty zombies, I start running out of creative names and just call them *asshole.* It seems that as long as I'm insulting, these zombies will follow me anywhere.

Must be a Viking thing.

Next I lead them all into the outpost. You know those clown cars where a ton of folks fit into a small spot? That's how it works with the Draugar and this building. I'd feel guilty for piling them in there, but they're all dead. What do they care?

In short order, I'm standing by the outpost door while shouting the word, *asshole* over and over. Once the last Draugar has crawled inside, Lincoln steps up.

"What's the deal?" I ask.

"Aaargh!" the zombies cry.

I roll my eyes. "Gah. They're so high maintenance. ASSHOLE ASSHOLE ASSHOLE! That make you happy?" Sure enough, the Draugar quiet down. I refocus on Lincoln. "Go on."

"None of our charms are working, but I was able to

glom some stuff together and make a bomb." He looks at the outpost and then to me. "Unfortunately, they aren't attacking us, so it would be unethical to destroy them."

"Oh, I can handle that." I open the door a crack. "You guys are the sweetest!"

Multiple hands reach for my throat. "KILL KILL KILL!"

"Works for me," says Lincoln. He tosses what looks like a mushed-up pile of junk into the outpost, slams the door shut and grabs my hand. I don't need any instructions for the next part of the plan.

I run my ass off. We're only ten yards away when Lincoln curls his body over mine.

KABOOM! The entire outpost explodes.

Things hit the nearby ground with a series of ominous plops. I try not to think about it too much. And now that the excitement is over, the smell of dumpster juice is making me way sick. I don't want to know what the sight of random body parts will do.

"Do you think I can get to the temple without opening my eyes?" I ask Lincoln.

"Definitely." He scoops me up and carries me off.

13

LINCOLN

Keeping Myla in my arms, I speed along the cobblestone path.

My thoughts spin through everything that's happened during the last few minutes. None of it seems real. Myla just went toe-to-toe with a zombie who was wielding a meat cleaver. My wife literally got that Draugar in line, along with the rest of them.

After about a quarter mile, the path abruptly ends. The building before me is a square structure made of white marble and colored tiles. Pillars surround the exterior. That's a temple, all right.

I curl Myla more closely against my chest. "We're here. Are you ready?"

"I'm good."

I set her on her feet. Myla scans the building, just as I did. "This is really something."

"Agreed."

"I mean, if I needed to hide a golden tree somewhere, it would be inside a temple like this one."

My heart soars. "You know, you might just be right."

TEMPLE

14

MYLA

*L*incoln and I march up the main stairs and into the temple proper. My stomach's still not great after the Great Draugar Encounter. I'm hoping the purple sand situation inside the temple will be better. Someone must know how to use a broom around here, right?

No such luck. There's violet stuff all over this floor, too.

I scan the rest of the space carefully. Intricate murals cover the walls—it's a *who's who* of Norse monsters. There's the fossegrim swamp guy, a battle dwarf and even some cute little elves.

Another archway leads outside. There's no missing the rustling noises from that space. My pulse speeds. Someone's definitely here.

Lincoln nods toward the exit arch and frowns. The question is there. *Are you up for this?*

Ignoring my nasty tummy, I give my guy a hearty thumbs-up. *Oh yeah.*

Together, Lincoln and I step over to the opposite archway and pause. Turns out, this exit leads to a small balcony and a tall elf.

She's tall, lithe and lovely in a saffron dress that perfectly offsets her chocolate-colored skin. Her ears point upward in the classic look of elves everywhere.

And I thought the Draugar thing was unexpected.

SENTINEL

MYLA

"*I* am the Sentinel, Leader of the Light Elves and Protector of Underland." The woman has a musical voice that totally matches her general elfyness. And since she leads her people, it explains why she's a lot taller than the child-like folks I saw on the temple walls.

I'm about introduce myself when my stomach decides that now is a good time to feel sick as fuck. So I keep my mouth shut. Thankfully, Lincoln manages the intros.

"I am King Lincoln. This is Queen Myla. We're in search of the Golden Apples of Idunn."

Something nasty-tasting crawls up my throat. *This isn't going well.*

"Hey." I wave toward the Sentinel. "Question for

you. Do you mind if I stand next to you? Because it looks like someone got around to sweeping your balcony area, and I'll feel much better if I'm off this purple stuff."

"Better?" She tilts her head. "What do you mean?"

I don't reply with words. Instead, I lean over and barf my guts out. I'm talking major heaving and everything. Yes, there's even some splatter on the Sentinel's super-pretty dress.

Fuuuuuuuuuuuuck.

On the plus side, the Sentinel's elfy eyes are all wide with sympathy. I'm taking that as approval for my *step onto the balcony plan.* So I sashay around my own sick and stand beside her.

"Hoo." I pat my tummy. "I'm still a little nauseous, but it's much better here." I make a wincey-face. "Sorry about your dress."

The Sentinel gestures across her gown. Purple sparkles tumble from her fingertips and settle on the fabric. The moment the violet particles touch her skirts, the gown cleans itself.

I lift my brows. "That's some handy magic."

"My powers reach through both Underland and Lower Gurith," states the Sentinel. "I've been listening to you two since you stepped out of the Pulpitum. The news about your pregnancy is most welcome."

To emphasize that point, a gentle breeze swoops past us, complete with little purple sparkles.

"Thanks for understanding." I try to say that in my most queenly voice. But it's only been a few days since I got my crown, so the tone comes out a lot like my regular voice. *Whatever.*

Suddenly, my tail starts bobbing at double speed. "Oh, one more thing. My tail wants to say hello."

The Sentinel bows slightly. "Greetings, Myla's Tail."

Instead of acting supercool, my tail bobs at an even faster speed. *Ugh.* The thing can be such an attention hound.

The Sentinel frowns. "What does Myla's Tail want?"

I'd make up a lie, but I've already barfed on this lady's dress."Just give it a compliment."

"You have lovely black scales," says the Sentinel.

Satisfied, my tail finally droops to hang out by my ankle.

The Sentinel turns to Lincoln. "My people owe yours a great debt. The House of Gurith brought us here many years ago."

Lincoln tilts his head. "What happened, exactly? We don't have any records of it."

"It is painful to recall, but you do need to know. Kell is a sort of Dark Elf called a marauder. His people use magic to set up Salients. I happened to be on the stretch of land that Kell decided to move to this reality. About a hundred of us were taken." She sighs. "One moment, we were in the Norse Universe. The next second, we found ourselves in a different reality ruled by ghouls."

"The ghouls couldn't have liked that," I declare.

"They didn't. They tried to attack, but Kell's magic killed them before they could even set foot on the Purple Salient. All the while, Kell enchanted us to do his bidding. My people built that arena for him. Beware of Kell's drums. If you aren't careful, that sound will force you into do anything he wants."

A memory appears. There were drums at the Viking Games. The sound didn't affect me, but it was my first game. The magic must build up over time.

"Then some thrax arrived," says the Sentinel. "They saw what happened and offered to fight in Kell's Arena. While they distracted Kell, we were able escape."

"That's a classic thrax operation," says Lincoln. "My people would have been called in once the ghouls were killed. I wonder why we have no records of it."

"I fear your thrax all died in the arena," states the Sentinel. "My people didn't have enough magic to return us to the Nordic Universe, but your thrax kindly gave us instructions to find this place. Over time, we used our powers to build things up to resemble our homeland." She looks at the trees over the balcony's edge. "Antrum gives us some protection, yet we are not free from Kell."

"You're talking about the Draugar," says Lincoln. "The Ringmaster must have set them up to prevent anyone else from finding you."

The Sentinel nods. "A handful of thrax have ventured near Underland. None were warriors. The Draugar frightened them away."

This story is definitely getting good. "What about the Golden Apples of Idunn? When you moved here from the Dark Lands, was the tree brought along?"

"In a way," says the Sentinel. "When we first came to this place, we pled to the goddess Idunn for mercy. Her sacred tree appeared. For three days, we tried to climb the trunk and pluck a golden apple. None of us could. The tree vanished. Idunn protects women warriors, which by definition includes mothers. Now that you are here, I am confident Idunn's tree will appear once more."

Hope sparks in my chest. "That's great news. Let's just hit that tree and get this over with. I know each apple gives a wish, so I'll grab two—one for us and one for you."

"Thank you." The Sentinel frowns.

"You don't seem too pleased about that offer," says Lincoln.

"We are still part of the Norse Universe," explains the Sentinel. "Moving here didn't break our connection to Kell. The ringmaster doesn't know you two are in Underland, but that cannot last for long. My people have little magic. If the ringmaster comes here, we cannot protect you from him. And when Kell decides someone does not belong on the purple sand…" She leaves the logic out there.

I finish off her statement. "They suffer the same fate as the ghoul army."

The Sentinel nods. "I'm afraid so."

Lincoln focuses on the Sentinel. "You know Kell better than anyone. The ringmaster is obsessed with making the Viking Games as perfect as possible. What if a new warrior showed up and offered to join? Would that distract him from Myla?"

"It might," says the Sentinel. "Distraction is a far better plan than fighting the ringmaster on Norse soil. Are you proposing to join the Viking Games?"

"Perhaps," answers Lincoln. "Myla and I need to talk first."

The Sentinel nods. "Of course."

I shoot her a thumbs-up. "We'll be fast."

And I mean it.

LINCOLN

*M*yla and I step back into the main rotunda of the temple. The moment we're alone, I cup her face in my hands.

"Are you feeling all right?"

"My tummy's relatively fine."

I pull her into a deep hug. "Good." Leaning back, I scan her features carefully. "What do you think of the Sentinel? Do you trust her?"

"I do," says Myla. "I mean, she's living in a freaking cave and wants to go home to her own reality. I don't think she's pretending they have an apple tree when they don't."

"Agreed."

For a moment, it's just me, Myla and the special

magic that always happens when we're alone. This is a horrible situation and yet, we're both smiling.

Both our grins slowly fade. When I speak, my voice is low and husky. "I wish I could stay."

Myla lower lip wobbles. "I know you need to leave." She gestures across her mouth. "Don't mind the lip action going on here. It's just hormones. Stupid magical pregnancy."

Suddenly, all signs of sorrow vanish from Myla's face. Her tail arcs over her shoulder as her eyes flare with a red light. I've heard about mood swings during pregnancy. Guess this is what they look like.

"Just know this," declares Myla. "I am *not* raising this baby alone. My mother had to do it and it made her nuts. So if you get killed, I am using my Scala powers to shove your soul back into your body, zombie-style."

How I love this woman. "That's a very reasonable solution. And if I become a zombie, then I promise not to eat your brains."

Myla exhales slowly. "Glad we cleared that up."

I gently rest my palm against her stomach. "You two stay safe."

It's the most natural and painful thing in the world to fall into another embrace. Neither of us begins or ends the hug. It just happens.

Somehow, I'm able to press a gentle kiss to Myla's forehead and walk away.

MYLA

*L*incoln hoists the pack on his shoulder and marches out the front archway. For a hot second, I debate about watching him step through the mists of Underland until his form disappears into the shadows.

Then I decide that's a crap idea.

I suck at goodbyes. Watching Lincoln leave while boohooing under an archway… that doesn't seem like a good use of my time. For now, Lincoln is gone. The sooner I find myself some golden apples, the faster we can get back to our honeymoon.

My mouth still tastes like I licked my old high school cafeteria floor, so I unzip my backpack and take a sip from the canteen. Then I take out a Demon Bar.

Comfort food, come to Momma.

While biting off my first chunk of yum, I head back to the balcony and Sentinel.

"Sorry we made you wait," I call. "Lincoln and I had to talk."

Once again, I cross the threshold. Another unexpected sight greets me.

There's no Sentinel.

I set my fists on my hips. *Huh.* This is a balcony and the Sentinel is a magical being. Maybe she just enchanted some wings and flew off to check on a unicorn or something.

I'll give her a minute.

I give it all of thirty seconds.

After shoving the rest of the Demon Bar into my mouth at once, I dive into my backpack and pull out my charmed walkie-talkie. I press the button. "Lincoln?"

No signal.

I press a lot more buttons, but the device stays dead. Not that I was too hopeful in the first place. Lincoln tried a ton of stuff when we were fighting the Draugar. Nothing worked then, either.

Now, I did tell Lincoln that I trust the Sentinel. But that was before she poofed her ass off the balcony without even saying goodbye.

Talk about your red flags.

To add an *upper bun* onto this particular shit sandwich, I don't even have the enchanted runestone to use as a compass. It's still with Lincoln. For a long minute, I shift my weight from foot to foot and consider my options.

Fuck it. I'm out of here.

Hoisting up my pack, I march out the front archway of the temple and take off in the direction of the super-squeezy passage back to Lower Gurith.

I don't get far before something odd happens.

My tail goes berserk. It takes different shapes—I'm talking zigzag, corkscrew, you name it—all while pointing toward the heart of Underland.

That would be the opposite direction of where I want to go.

"Cut it out," I warn my tail. "In case you forgot, I have *the feet* in this relationship, so you'll just have to adjust."

I try marching *away* from Underland, but my tail is being creative in its destruction. It stops trying to drag me off. Instead, it takes to spearing its arrowhead end into local scenery including a tree, shrub and large mushroom.

"I'm not stopping. I've got the legs too, bitch."

My tail moves onto a new strategy, the little sneak. It's called The Let's Trip Myla Up Scheme. Sadly, this plan is pretty effective. I fall on my ass twice before I give up.

Rising, I rub my right butt cheek and start to negotiate. "What do you want?"

My tail gestures wildly towards the heart of Underland.

"You want to go find the Sentinel?"

This time, my tail arcs around so the arrowhead-shaped end points right at my nose. It then goes into a slow bobbing routine that's its version of sarcastic nod.

"Okay, your plan was pretty obvious." I sigh. "And you really think this is a good idea?"

More bobbing follows, only of the *far more vigorous* variety.

I stick out my tongue in a combo *yuck-n-boo* face. "Are you sure you can find her?"

My tail flips around so I see the 'back' of its arrowhead face.

"There's no need to get pissy."

The end flips around again and sways from side to side. It's a dead-on impression the head movements I always make when I tell it to avoid having a pissy-tude.

Does my tail know me or what? I am clearly losing this fight. Best to give in to the inevitable.

"You're right. I shouldn't have doubted you."

My tail's arrowhead end angles toward the depths of Underland. The meaning is clear.

That way, already.

I reset the pack on my shoulders and take off in the direction my tail indicates. As I walk along, the arrowhead end bops around in its own version of a happy dance.

I can only hope it knows what it's doing.

LINCOLN

Marching away from the temple, I make a beeline for the place Myla called the *squeezy tunnel*. Once I'm through that passage, I'll return to Lower Gurith. From there, I can use a transfer charm to reach the Dark Lands.

In short order, I'm stepping off the Pulpitum and onto the Phantom Forest. A crowd streams around me. Everyone's on their way to the Viking Games.

On the way over here, I also put on a ring of obfuscation. Now, none of my people will recognize their king. The charm only works for an hour, but that should be long enough for me to find Kell.

As I march over to the arena, I pull out my human-looking walkie talkie, press the button on the side and speak a secret code into the microphone.

"Aquilineans eternal."

Then I wait.

It doesn't take long for the device to spark to life. As I'd hoped, Walker's deep voice sounds over the small speaker. "Why am I hearing from you? You're supposed to be on your honeymoon."

"One moment, I need to step away from the crowd."

While I find a quiet place to talk, the speaker crackles to life again. "I take it back, you're married to Myla Lewis. Of course, something's wrong. That girl is a whirlwind of trouble."

"And thank Heaven for it. Life was exceedingly tedious before she arrived. Although in this case, the trouble comes from a different source." I scan the area. I've stepped into a copse of trees. No one is within listening distance. "Myla is pregnant."

"Congratulations." Walker pauses. "Wait, how is that a bad thing?"

"Because Connor has made an unbreakable deal with ringmaster Kell to have my son fight in the Viking Games. Father believes that the Purple Salient will keep his grandson safe from the King of Hell."

"I should have guessed it." Walker groans. "After the wedding, Connor went on and on about the threat from Armageddon. Kell's land is technically not part of the after-realms, so it would give protection from the King of Hell."

"Correct."

"So what's your plan?"

"Myla must find some magical items called the Golden Apples of Idunn. She can wish on them to end Connor's arrangement. Meanwhile, I'll go to the Viking Arena and stall Kell."

"Do you need help from the Aquilineans?"

"Absolutely."

Both Walker and I are descended from the archangel Aquila. Her descendants are expert warriors. Walker runs the ghoul faction.

"Get as many Aquilineans together as you can," I continue. "Infiltrate the audience at the Viking Games and stay alert. And whatever you do, keep this a secret. Officially, Myla and I are still camping."

"And what about Connor's arrangement with Kell? Surely, Octavia must know about it."

"She doesn't. When Father wants to keep a secret, he's got some serious skills."

"No doubt." Static sounds from the speaker before Walker speaks once more. "It'll take some time to round up the Aquilineans. I better run."

"Thanks, Walker."

The walkie talkie goes dead. A weight of worry slips

from my shoulders. Things will go better with Walker on the job.

Although something tells me that Kell has some secret help of his own.

Straightening my shoulders, I take off for the Arena.

Time to face the ringmaster.

LINCOLN

I march right into the Viking Arena. The show is mostly over, so no one's even checking tickets.

Works for me.

Inside, the arena is a bowl-like structure that's lined with benches. A wide outer hall encircles the seating area. This way, the audience can find their places without leaving the arena proper. As I walk along, I check the various access passages.

I'm about halfway around when I see something unexpected.

The ringmaster.

Through this thin hallway, I can make out both the regular Kell... as well as the giant version inside the arena itself.

"Tonight, we present two new warriors," says Giant Kell. "They go by the fighting names of Wrecker and Pulverizer!" The crowd cheers. "These thrax will now take a vow to serve the Viking Games forever."

While this goes on, I step into the passageway. Up close, it's clear that the real Kell isn't even mouthing the words from his massive counterpart. The only sign that he's manipulating anything is the way his fingers twitch to puppeteer the action.

That's some serious magic.

Little by little, Kell turns his head and focuses directly at me. There's no malice in his eyes… only indifference. He looks away.

Worry twists through me. After all, the guy is kidnapping my son. You'd think he'd be concerned to find me sneaking up on him in a darkened passageway.

Straightening my spine, I march over to stand beside Kell. For a moment, I soak in a full view of the arena. The seats are mostly empty. No wonder Kell thought this would be a safe place to hang out. There are no spectators to step past and wonder why the ringmaster is human-sized.

Down on the arena floor, the purple sands bubble and heave. A humanoid rodent rises from the ground. The ratatoskr. A drumbeat rises through the air. Kell flicks his fingers with minuscule motions as he controls the battle.

It doesn't go well.

The Wrecker and Pulverizer are bulky but untrained. When you're fighting a foe like a ratatoskr, you must be agile. Bulging muscles just get in the way.

Suddenly, it strikes me that Kell might not be indifferent to me so much as distracted. It isn't easy to puppeteer other people. Which means that now is an excellent time to try and strike a deal.

"I'm here to talk," I begin.

"We've nothing to discuss." Reaching into his pocket, Kell pulls out his own version of the runestone. "I already own your son. Leave me."

My mind whirs through options. There must be some way I can grab Kell's interest and keep the conversation going.

"This fight is pitiful," I declare.

Kell shoots me an angry glance. "That's a lie."

What a strong reaction. *Just what I need.* Myla is an expert at using anger to help her focus. The wild look in Kell's eyes tell me he doesn't have that skill.

"Come now," I continue. "Even with your magical puppeteering, there's only so much you can do. This isn't a battle; it's a rout. The crowd's already leaving. You need better warriors to take on a ratatoskr."

"It's just an off night." Kell shrugs. "One battle doesn't mean anything."

Myla and I spent a lot of time reading up on the history of the Norse Universe. That said, we didn't look into how many people were actually attending Kell's games. Right now, that looks like a big miss.

Is this truly an off night? Who knows?

At this point, there is only one thing to do. Bluff like Hell.

"Please. We both know your magic isn't infinite. You've been losing your touch for years. Everyone knows it. Why else would you agree to possibly take on Armageddon and protect my son?"

If Kell were a porcupine, his quills would be up and ready to deploy. "What of it?"

"You once gave me a chance to fight in the arena. Does the offer still stand? Combine my fighting skills with your magic, and we could put on a real show."

Kell eyes me carefully. His look of rage melts into one of interest. "Would you really do that?"

"I'll step in and fight the ratatoskr... but only if you break your vow with Connor."

Kell steps closer. "Win three games *including* this one and I will end that bargain."

I frown. Kell agreed to that awfully easily. "How do I know you'll keep you word?"

"You're strong enough in angelic power to cast an unbreakable blood vow. Speak the incantation and see for yourself. Magic won't allow me to make promises I can't keep."

Outside, I maintain my mask of calm. Inside, I'm churning. There must be a catch. A memory appears. The Sentinel warned me about Kell's drums. The ringmaster must think I'll give into his will before four games are over.

"I have some conditions, Kell. I won't speak the same vow that your fighters do. That means I'll never promise to serve the arena forever."

"Agreed."

So far, so good.

"And I don't want to listen to those drums of yours. Give me protection from the noise."

"I'm afraid that's impossible. No drums, no vow." Kell narrows his eyes. "What made you change your mind about joining the games, anyway? Have you been exploring in Lower Gurith?"

My stomach sinks. Whatever happens, I can't allow Kell to figure out what Myla's doing. I'll just have to take my chances with Kell's enchanted drums.

"Our focus needs to be here, not on Antrum," I announce. "Here's my offer. I'll win you four total games, including this one against the ratatoskr. I will not take your warrior's vow. You will allow me to keep my thrax charms." Here I lift my backpack to show what I mean. "In exchange, you'll break the deal with Connor."

"I'll take that bargain." Kell rubs his palms together. "Imagine what I could do with a warrior of your skill. I may need to hire more ghouls to work the ticket booths."

I fight the urge to sigh with relief. Kell is now focused on what happens when I fight in his arena. All thoughts of Lower Gurith are gone.

Time to make the magic happen.

Pulling out my baculum, I ignite the rods into a dagger. With careful movements, I cut a line across my own palm. Next I do the same to Kell. Tapping into my angelic nature, I speak a Latin incantation that will bind us to our promises.

As I finish speaking, both our palms sparkle with power. The spell begins. Not that I should be surprised. Blood vows are the most powerful magic around. As the light fades, blue marks appear on the back of our hands. Each image shows a Viking hammer.

The spell is cast.

Kell grins. "See? Blood magic doesn't lie. I will break

my bargain with Connor if you win four games." The ringmaster lifts his hand. Purple light flares out from his palm. When the brightness fades, Kell now grips a helmet. He offers me the gear.

"Take this. All my warriors must hide their face and take a stage name."

I set the helm upon my head. It's not the best in the after-realms, but I've worn worse. "This will do."

"And what's your stage name?"

"Don't you want everyone to know I'm a king?"

"And have half the after-realms try to invade my arena? Your mother alone is enough reason for secrecy. No, I don't wish to erase whole armies of potential customers. Not if I can avoid it, anyway."

I narrow my eyes as I take in this turn of events. Kell knows Mother is still unaware of his deal with Connor. Again, those are some impressive skills.

Kell continues. "As I said, what name do you want? Most folks already have something locked away in their hearts." He leans in closer. "Hasn't some little part of you always wanted to be in the Viking Games? Give me a name."

"You pick one for me."

"As you command."

Kell snaps his fingers. Purple sand already covers the arena floor. Now those violet particles bubble up around my feet. Moments later, I'm pulled under the earth. Darkness follows. Seconds pass before I find myself rising again. Only this time, I'm not standing in a passageway with Kell, but on the battle floor itself.

Wrecker and Pulverizer are gone. Now it's just me and the ratatoskr.

Ratatoskr

LINCOLN

I trained to fight in the human world. My battles take place in grocery stores. High-ways. Forests. You name it. The demons I go up against love to camouflage themselves. They'll glom onto panes of glass in the frozen foods aisle. Or curl up inside floodlights along a busy intersection. Some even attach themselves to the backs of unsuspecting park rangers.

My current fight is nothing like that.

I stand at one side of a long oval arena. Sand slides beneath my boots. Far off on the other side, there paces the raratoskr. A real predator would move back and forth as a way to relieve tension. All the while, it would use its gaze either to intimidate or assess.

That's not what's happening here.

The ratatoskr stares blindly ahead as it races, leaps

and flips. Every so often, it lets out a rat-like squeal or claws at the ground. All this is meant to impress the crowd, not me.

The projected form of Ringmaster Kell stands in the center of the arena floor. From the audience's point of view, it's as if Kell is keeping me and the ratatoskr apart. In reality, my opponent is little more than a marionette. I'm not sure where the real Kell stands, but I've no doubt that he's the one pulling the strings here.

Taking out my baculum, I toss the silver rods between my hands. So far, Giant Kell has kept me in the shadows while he talks about the history of the games and what a special treat is coming tonight. All the while, spotlights rove across the ratatoskr, giving perfect flashes to every crowd-pleasing somersault and swipe.

"Ladies and gentlemen!" calls Giant Kell. "The time has come for our ground-breaking event of the evening. You shall now witness a first in the history of the Viking Games. We will not have a father-son team fight our next monster. I repeat, our next warrior will fight alone."

The crowd boos. I get the feeling they weren't happy at how Wrecker and Pulverizer were yanked off the battle floor. Some folks trudge up the exit aisles. Humans like leave early to avoid traffic. For thrax, the goal is to miss the Pulpitum lines.

"Do not despair!" cries Kell. "It's only fair for our next fighter to go in solo. That's because this warrior has skills that are so powerful and unique, the Viking Games has never seen the likes of him before."

A spotlight blasts in my direction. Fresh boos fill the air. A few audience members in the lower seats throw empty popcorn boxes and mead jugs in my direction. Voices pummel me as well.

"Get off the floor!"

"Bring back Wrecker and Pulverizer!"

"You're no warrior!"

It's the last phrase that does it. My temper rises. I picture my baculum becoming a long sword. The weapon flares to life in my hands.

One thing about angelfire—it shines with Heavenly brightness. Although I have a half-dozen spotlights on me, they're nothing compared to the fiery blade I now wield.

The crowd falls silent.

I'd worry about the quiet, but no one is throwing trash in my direction, either physically or verbally. This is a definite improvement.

Giant Kell gestures toward me. "Our new solo fighter is called… Baculum!"

Slow drumbeats fills the air. The audience claps in

time with the rhythm as it goes faster and faster. Soon the arena is a cacophony of cheers and pounding.

Giant Kell raises his arms. "Let the games begin!" His massive form blinks out of existence.

A question arises. In any battle, you can tell a lot by who makes the first strike. Are you trying to wear out your opponent? Lure them into hitting first? There's often a pause where both sides wait to see who starts.

Not so in this battle. The ratatoskr falls to all fours and races across the arena floor. Its claws tear through the ground, sending tiny plumes of sand behind it as it goes.

There are no false starts or zagging to hide its attack vector. As the ratatoskr closes in, it telegraphs its position by leaping into the air with its claws out and gleaming in the spotlights.

The drumbeats swell. I have the urge to swoop my baculum in a long arc and take off the creature's arm. This isn't my desire, though. It's something from outside me.

From Kell.

The ringmaster is trying to pull my puppet strings. I won't let that happen.

Instead, I extinguish my baculum and reset them in my holster. As the ratatoskr closes in, I step to one side, grab its arm and swing it across the arena floor. My opponent slides across the sand to slam into a barrier wall, knocking it unconscious. The crowd cheers.

For my part, I cross the arena floor, step under an access arch, and enter a long passage. Behind me, Giant Kell announces the end of the battle.

Surprisingly, I meet the real Kell in the shadowy hallway. He does not look pleased.

"You disobeyed my commands," states the ringmaster.

"Did you expect something else?"

Kell's eyes flare with rage. "Next time, you'll listen. For now, you need to settle in. The lower levels are down this passage. Don't bother trying to leave. You cannot step outside arena while our agreement is active. My magic won't allow it."

"I'd no intention of going." Mostly because I want to stay and keep distracting Kell. Not that I'll share that part out loud.

"Good. Pick your own bed." He shoots me a sinister grin. "And sleep well."

I stalk away, wondering what the Hell I've gotten myself into.

21

LINCOLN

*L*eaving the arena floor behind, I step down a ramp and into a warren of subterranean passages. One thing about growing up in Antrum—I always find my way underground.

As I explore the many chambers, I don't run across anyone else. Even so, I do catch the low murmur that means others wait nearby. Knowing that, I take care to move in the opposite direction. Why? My only chance to defeat Kell's mind control is to limit my interactions with his world. I won't eat his food, talk to his warriors, or listen to his drums. For that last bit, I already have a silencer charm in my backpack.

This bargain can work. I'll make it happen.

I meander around until I find an area that's marked for new warriors… And it's totally deserted. *Perfect.*

It's soon clear why no one wants to stay here. The place is more of a prison than anything else. Not a problem. I pick a cell that's the most isolated and set myself up. The room only holds a cot and side table. Rays of permanent—and false—sunlight stream through the window. Heavy drumbeats fill the air.

Opening my backpack, I get to my first order of business. That would be taking out my silencer charm—which is a hefty ring set with an azure stone—and placing it upon my thumb. Once that's done, absolute quiet surrounds me. Next I eat some canned stew and try to rest.

Unfortunately, I spend most of the night staring at the ceiling while contemplating the core riddle of the ringmaster. Kell could use his magic to achieve any goal. Why is he so obsessed that everything in his Viking Games be perfect?

Yet no matter how much I turn that question over in my mind, I never do find any answers.

WARRIOR CELL

22

MYLA

*O*nce I leave the temple, I spend lots of quality time getting led around by my tail. The scenery is pretty, but my ass is killing me. After about eight hours of this, I come to a major decision.

No matter what, I *am* finding the Sentinel.

And when I do discover her hiding place, the Sentinel is getting a piece of my mind. Who runs off and leaves someone standing? Sheesh.

When darkness falls, I set up my own camp. It's not too hard. Now that the Dräugar are toast, there's no nasty sense of menace in the air.

I wake up, choke down my stew, and hear a strange noise.

Someone's crying.

This time, I don't even need my tail to lead me around. I follow the sound and find a little creature sitting on a stone. She's a child-like thing with curly horns on her forehead and gossamer wings on her back. All in all, she looks like the light elf I saw on the walls of the temple.

"I hurt my foot," she says. "Can you help?"

I look over my shoulder, wondering if there's anyone elfy behind me. *There isn't.*

"You mean me?" I ask.

"Yes, you. Myla Lewis. You're the one with the back-pack full of charms. It isn't fair that you have so many."

Her words rattle around my mind. There's some-thing important in her attitude. Try as I might, I can't quite place it.

My tail takes the opportunity to pop up and wave. Ack. I should have expected this.

"Hello, Myla's tail," says the elf.

Whoa. That's the second time this elf said my name. Did she use magic to find out who I am… or did she get a heads-up on my identity from the Sentinel? I'm guessing it's the second thing.

"You know my name." I step closer. "What's yours?"

"Rustle." She lifts her chin. "I'm the latest sacrifice."

"Okay."

Not sure what a *sacrifice* means here, but I'm guessing this chick can help me find the Sentinel.

Oh, yeah.

RUSTLE

23

MYLA

I blink hard, trying to process what's happening. It isn't easy. Before me, a light elf keeps pointing at her owie toe. I open my mouth, trying to come up with something funny—or at least super sarcastic—to add to the situation.

I got nothing.

"Didn't you hear what I said?" asks Rustle. "I'm the sacrifice."

"I did."

"Aren't you going to ask me what that means?"

"Okay, I'll bite. What does it mean?"

"I'm *not* going to tell you."

"Color me not-shocked."

My trash mouth might be malfunctioning, but the rest of my brain is working fine. Fortunately, I read about light elves in Lincoln's library. They act like a demon whose fuckery I know quite well.

The fabula.

Fabulas are lovely as movie stars and mean as snakes. They'll steal your life force if you're not careful. To deal with a fabula, you must follow the same three rules as with a light elf.

First, a fabula might offer you food. Never eat it (unless you want to get enchanted).

Second, fabulas also play lots of verbal games, like how Rustle having me ask about sacrifices. *Ignore it.*

Third, never take a deal from a fabula, but make bargains when you can. *They do keep their word.*

And the fact that Rustle wanted me to ask a question she knew she wouldn't answer? Classic fabula.

"My foot hurts. Open your backpack and help me."

"Sure, I can cure you, but I need something first."

"Yes, let's form a covenant. I'll give you terms."

Ha. Like that will happen.

Rule number four: always be super specific with fabulas and elves. Otherwise, they'll find some way to screw you over.

"No, I'll do that part. If I heal your foot, then you must take me to the Sentinel."

"I agr—"

"No wait, there's more. You'll transport me to the Sentinel."

"We don't transport in Underland. We walk and fly."

"Fine. You'll *walk* me to the Sentinel—"

"So rude. Flying is easier."

"But I don't have wings. Plus, you'll walk me there at a regular pace with reasonable breaks for me to go the bathroom or whatever. Is it a deal?"

Rustle sighs dramatically. "I agree." She waves her arm and pretty emerald sparkles fly through the air. "Our covenant is set."

She laughs her little ass off. "I won! I won!"

"That's usually my line."

"The Sentinel asked me to find you. You bargained away nothing."

"News flash." I do jazz hands to emphasize my point. "I would have helped you for nothing, so we're even."

Rustle puffs out her lower lip. "Oh."

Opening my backpack, I fish around for what looks like lip balm. It's really an all-purpose haling charm. Stepping up to Rustle, I check out her foot. One of her toes is pretty mashed up.

"How did you do this?" I ask.

She winks. "I don't remember."

"Because you're the sacrifice for the lost light elves… only you won't tell me anything about that."

She giggles. "Of course, not."

"Ha, ha."

I set the tube against her toe. The moment it touches her skin, the charm glows with blue light. *Angelic power.* The colorful energy then moves into Rustle's body. Within seconds, her toe is healed.

Rustle hops down from her rock. "Now, I'll take you to the Sentinel. But before we go, please let me do something for you to show my appreciation." Rustle clasps her hands under her chin while blinking madly. "Perhaps you want to eat some mushrooms? I know which ones are yummy."

Let the record show that I use the *innocent blinking routine* myself. But adding in the hands clasping? That's new.

"Nuh-uh," I reply.

"So is that a *no*?"

"Correct. I will never, ever eat mushrooms from you."

Rustle flits closer. "Does that backpack hold your food?"

"Yes."

"Can I carry it for you?"

"So you can ruin it somehow? No."

Rustle flies around in a circle while laughing hysterically. "You're no fun."

"Get walking," I state. To emphasize the point, my tail gestures toward a particular break in the trees.

"Oh, my! Your tail already knows how to reach the Sentinel. Why do you need me anyway?"

"Because you're both light elves and wicked tricksy. The Sentinel already disappeared on me once. You've spent most of our time together playing games. I'm not letting you loose from your promise until I'm face to face with the Sentinel again."

"Yes, your Majesty!" Rustle goose steps off toward the trees. I follow along, careful to watch her every movement. Behind me, my tail bobs happily.

At least one of us is having a good time.

24

LINCOLN

*W*hen I finally do fall asleep, I dream that I've returned to the wedding reception for me and Myla. Everything spins around me, plastic and intense. Myla is near and I experience her as a kaleidoscope of sensation. I catch the flash of blue light in her eyes… feel the brush of her fingertips on my neck… and inhale her unique scent of cinnamon and sunshine.

Suddenly, the room darkens. New music fills the air. The gentle waltz transforms into a cascade of pounding drums. The smell of roasted meat overwhelms my senses. I search for Myla, but the ballroom is filled with strangers.

A child wails. I push through the crowd to find a small boy huddled in the corner. I kneel before him.

"What's wrong?" I ask.

The child looks up. He's a five-year-old cherub with large blue eyes. He cuddles the end of his dragonscale tail to his chest. Tears stream down his cheeks. His mop of brown hair sticks up at odd angles.

In that moment, I know the truth. This is my son. It's Maxon.

"I want real sunshine, Daddy. I hate the Dark Lands."

I try to grasp Maxon's hands, but his little fingers always stay out of reach. "I'm trying to get you free."

Maxon sniffles. "Grandpa Connor didn't protect you. Now you can't keep me safe, either."

The ballroom becomes empty. The drums play faster as Maxon stays curled in a corner, only the walls of the chamber expand out, turning a small space into a massive one. I chase after my boy, but I can't make up the distance between us.

"Daddy, save me!"

I awaken with a gasp. Sitting up, I find myself back in my cell. Beads of sweat trickle down my spine. A table now sits beside my cot. It's laden with all the roasted meats, buttered vegetables, and sweets that I smelled in my dream. My mouth waters. I've never seen food that's more appetizing.

But I don't need to use a charm to confirm that every bite of this stuff is laden with Kell's magic.

The low thud of drums echoes all around me. I

frown. that can't be right. I knew Kell's drums were enchanted. That's why I set a silencer ring on my thumb before I went to sleep.

Raising my hand, I check out the ring. The main gemstone is cracked and gray. Worry twists across my neck and shoulders. This silencer charm should have worked for a full day. I check my watch. It's 6:17 a.m.

The silencer charm didn't even last twelve hours.

When we passed into Underland, Myla said the purple sand affected her. I didn't sense it then, but now that I'm here and underground? I can feel the particles behind every wall and floorboard. The unique magic of the Norse Universe assaults my own powers. My skin prickles over with an ethereal chill.

I press my palms against my eyes. *Think, Lincoln.*

Myla will be here soon with the Golden Apple of Idunn… and that magical item will deliver a single wish. She'll ask for Connor's vow to end.

And then this entire nightmare will be over. I just have to wait.

The drumbeat grows louder. I pull another silencer ring from my backpack and set it on my thumb. Blissful quiet follows. I take in a series of slow breaths.

No question about it. I need to eat, wash, and get ready for my day. Before any of that, I drag the feasting table out into the hallway. Unless it comes from my own backpack, I'm not allowing it anywhere near my person.

And once I'm ready? I'll set off and find Kell.

The reason why is simple. I've no doubt that Myla is off finding that golden apple. I need to buy her time.

The more I can distract the ringmaster, the better for us all.

GRAND SOLAR

25

LINCOLN

With my silencer ring on, I can't hear the pounding drums. That said, I can still sense the sound waves in my chest. If my guess is right, I only have to follow that beat and it will lead me to the ringmaster.

Leaving my cell, I follow the pulses until I reach an elaborate chamber. The place is all plush carpets, intricate patterns, and fringed pillows. An enchanted window streams more false sunlight onto the scene.

As I walk inside, a roll of drums sound. I check my thumb ring. The new gemstone is already cracked. Which means another of my silencer charms are ruined. And this time it only took a matter of minutes. Damn.

A fresh chill rolls up my back as the cold prickle of Kell's magic slams into me. I turn around and, sure enough, he's there. His bulky form overwhelms the small space. The bold marks on his bare chest contrast with the intricate patterns everywhere else. I wonder if the room is built on a smaller scale to make Kell seem larger. I wouldn't be surprised.

"I call this room the Grand Solar." Kell sets his hands on his hips. "Did you see the windows? Notice how the sunbeams arc toward the floor. I bet you don't have anything like that in Antrum."

One thing I'll say for the Ringmaster. He's supremely competitive. We've spent less than a minute together, and already he wants to compare dicks over who has the better underground realm.

"Angelic magic protects Antrum. It gives us air to breathe, caves that don't collapse, and sends out diffuse light to match whatever is happening on the Earth's surface."

Kell lifts his chin. "So you don't have sunbeams like those from this window."

"No."

Kell locks onto my gaze. The ghost of a smirk rounds his mouth. He wants me to know that I just lost a battle.

For my part, I keep my face carefully neutral. There are many perks to being royalty. One negative is that you become a symbol to knock down, stand upon, or fawn over. In other words, this isn't the first time someone's tried to lure me into comparing realms with Antrum. It doesn't rile my soul.

"I'm so excited you're here," says Kell. "Together, we'll build up the Viking Games again." He gestures toward the door. "How about a tour of your new home?"

I arch my right brow. "I've only agreed to four games."

"Too afraid to spend the day with me?"

"Lead on."

In reality, I'd rather floss with barbed wire than waste more time with Kell. But touring the facility is a great chance to distract the ringmaster.

I'm taking it.

Kell has more than a few subterranean floors to this complex. Beneath the Viking Arena, Kell has created an underground skyscraper of levels and functions. Most places are as elaborate as the Grand Solar. We tour music rooms, dining areas, and libraries. At some point, the drums start up once more. The rooms begin to blur in my mind.

We're in yet another ornate dining chamber when Kell sets his hand on my shoulder. "Well, are you ready?"

Stepping back, I place some space between us. Kell's hand falls from my person.

"For what?" I ask.

"Why, the games are about to start."

I check my watch. Sure enough, it's almost 8 p.m. Kell and I couldn't have spent the entire day together. I check my watch once more. Still 8 p.m.

That bastard cast some kind of spell on my that toyed with my perception. It is indeed time for the games to begin. I pat the holster on my thigh, double-checking that my baculum are in place.

I fix Kell with a deadpan stare. "I'm always ready for battle."

The ringmaster smirks. We just played another game of magic and skills. This time, Kell won and he knows it.

Beneath my feet, the Persian carpet transforms into purple sand. The particles bubble and heave as I'm pulled into the ground.

Another battle is about to begin.

26

LINCOLN

Seconds later, I rise through the sands of the arena floor. Spotlights swoop across the scene. The crowd roars. Viking drums pound on the air. The massive version of the ringmaster looms above me.

"And the main event for the evening is about to begin," calls Giant Kell. "Tonight is the only fighter in the Viking Games to battle solo... the one and only... Baculum!"

The drums pound faster. The crowd cheers even louder.

"And tonight Baculum will fight an all-new opponent for the Viking Games... a unique monster from the Norse Universe... the jotnar!" With that, Giant Kell blinks out of existence.

The ground rumbles beneath my feet. Outside the

circle of spotlight, something massive rises to the surface. A pair of great arms reach toward me from the darkness. I take my baculum from their holster, ready to fight.

Because I know what's coming for me.

A Viking giant.

JOTNAR

27

LINCOLN

I stay at one side of the arena floor. All spotlights focus on me. The jotnar is kept in the shadows.

No doubt, Kell selected this particular opponent for a reason. I can't help but compare the jotnar and ratatoskr. A humanoid rodent should have been a wily fight. And I'm certain the battle looked great to the audience. But down on the arena floor? The creature telegraphed its every move. Or rather, Kell puppeteered the ratatoskr so poorly, my opponent's natural advantages were ruined.

All of which explains the choice of a jotnar.

Kell probably selected it to fix the ratatoskr's "mistakes." When you're an oversized behemoth, no one expects you to move quickly or conceal your intentions. The battle is won on sheer strength alone.

So Kell is adapting in an effort to beat me. These games may be more interesting than I expected.

At last, the jotnar fully lumbers into the spotlight. The audience gasps. Not that I blame them. This thing really is a beast. It stands about two stories tall with massive arms and legs. Each claw is as tall as I am.

Boom! Boom!

As the jotnar steps closer, the entire arena shakes. It lumbers forward in a direct line toward me. I pace from side to side, inspecting the creature from different angles. Calculations fly through my brain.

One fact quickly becomes clear.

This jotnar has an exceedingly small head. And I don't mean that to insult its intelligence. What I'm focused on are the possibilities for a *blood choke.* This is where you place pressure on the front arteries in your opponent's throat and cut off its blood supply. A chain reaction starts and no matter what your size, the same thing happens.

You pass out cold.

I nod once to myself, the decision made. *Jotnar, meet blood choke.*

My opponent is taking a while to cross the arena

floor, so I decide to bring the battle to him. While keeping my baculum in their holster, I race across the purple sand. Once I'm within range of the jotnar, it leans over to grab me.

How perfect.

Using my momentum, I fall into a slide and slip right between the creature's hands and legs. Once I'm behind the jotnar, I scale up its craggy back until reaching its neck. Then I wrap my right arm around its throat, while bolstering my grip with my left hand. Using all my strength, I put pressure on the front of the jotnar's neck.

The creature swats at me. That doesn't help. Then the jotnar slams its back against a nearby barrier wall. By angling out of the way at the last second, I narrowly avoid becoming royal roadkill.

By now, the lack of blood flow is becoming a problem for my opponent. It sways from foot to foot before falling over, unconscious.

As I leap away from the creature, I spot a familiar face in the audience. *Connor.* Blinking hard, I check again.

No, my father isn't here. And why would he visit the arena anyway? As far as Connor knows, Maxon is due to get carted off at birth. Myla and I are on a camping honeymoon. There's no reason to watch Viking Games from the cheap seats.

The crowd cheers. Drums sound. I saunter off the arena floor.

Two battles down, two to go.

LINCOLN

I march off the arena floor and into one of the exit archways. As I step along the darkened passage, the drums keep up their regular pounding. The beat turns so intense, my head feels as if it will explode.

All I want is to make a beeline for my cell. Sad as it is, that place is my only refuge in this arena. It holds my backpack—and the last tether to my life with Myla.

A trio of hooded ghouls step into my path, blocking me. I grasp my baculum, ready for battle.

Then I sigh.

These are Aquilineans. I step up to the tallest of the three.

"Walker." I grip his upper arm. "It's good to see you."

"My operatives just arrives. Do you have any orders?"

"Attend the games. Stay alert. Don't linger in the arena. The drums…" I shake my head.

Walker looks to his friends. "Divide up the audience into sectors. Assign owners. Move out." The other ghouls nod and step away.

Once Walker and I are alone, I scan his face. "Do you hear the drums?"

"Yes, but they don't effect me so much." His all-dark eyes widen with sympathy. "You've been here a long time. This must be hard for you."

"I'll manage."

Walker stares into the depths of the hallway. "You shouldn't stay there. The longer you remain, the harder it will get."

I straighten my shoulders. "I'm going back to my cell. There's work for me to do."

Walker frowns. "And how is that going?"

"I spent all day with Kell. Let's just say it was distracting for both of us."

Walker lowers his voice to a whisper. "I'm your friend. I won't lie to you." Even before Walker speaks the words, I know what he's going to say. "You don't look well. Are you sure you should wait for Myla?"

I straighten my spine and meet his gaze dead-on. "She's coming back with the golden apples of Idunn."

"Why risk your sanity? There may be some other way to fix this. We could bring in Xavier and Camilla."

"And start a war? No. I'm staying, Walker."

Walker sighs. "All right."

My friend reaches into the sleeves of his ghoul robes and pulls out eight silencer rings. Each one is encircled with blue gemstones. "This is as many as I could find."

"Thank you. The ones I brought only last a matter of minutes." I set the first ring onto my thumb. Blessed quiet descends around me.

Walker points to his chest and then to the access passageway. The meaning is clear. *Do you want me to go with you?*

I shake my head. "One of us needs to avoid the drums." I set the rings into my pocket. "Thank you for the charms."

Turning away, I march back toward my cell. Now that I have some peace, I must get some rest. After all, who knows how long these new silencer rings will last?

29

MYLA

Today is another fiesta of hiking with Rustle, AKA the world's most annoying elf.

Case in point. Rustle spent all morning asking if I would be willing to bargain away my youth, soul, or demon patrol charms in exchange for some sketchy-looking bits of mushroom. Mostly, she really wants my backpack.

Normally, I'd enjoy the chance to sass off at someone for hours on end. But I'm still dealing with the dual challenges of morning sickness and thigh chafe. Let's just say I'm not in the mood.

It isn't until the fiftieth time Rustle whines about how it isn't fair that I won't trade my backpack when it hits me.

In fact, the realization is so huge, it stops me right in my tracks.

"You're an envy elf."

Rustle takes to the skies to hover above me. I've learned that she often flies when feeling defensive. "How did you know that? It's not fair."

"I'm a quasi demon. My people are mostly human with a little demonic DNA. That gives us awesome tails." And because my tail is a total ham, it arches over my shoulder to wave at Rustle.

"Hello, Myla's Tail."

Side note. Let the record show that Rustle has a major fan in my tail. That doesn't happen often.

"But there's more to it than just having an amazing tail," I continue. "I also wield power across two sins, lust and wrath. For my best friend, Cissy, it's envy."

Rustle narrows her eyes. "What's she like?"

"Super loyal. Kind hearted. Crazy smart. And sure, she gets jealous easily, but it also means that she notices everything. You'd be surprised how often that comes in handy." I step closer. "Is that why you wear green?"

Rustle nods quickly.

I tap my chin. "The Sentinel wore yellow. Is that the color of wrath?"

More nodding. "She's the only wrath elf in Underland. The Sentinel happened to be visiting our village when Kell sent us here. The rest of my people are all envy and pride elves."

"Know what? That's the first time you said something that wasn't about my stuff. So Kell imprisoned you all here. Damn, do I ever know how that feels. For most of my life, my people were trapped by the ghouls."

Rustle and I share a sad smile. An invisible cord of connection winds between us. Suddenly, I realize we've spent hours together and I still don't know the answers to some basic questions about her.

"Why did the Sentinel send you after me?"

Rustle lifts her chin. "I wasn't sent; I volunteered. Sure, my foot was hurt, but I could still fly. And you might have outsider magic that would help me heal."

"There's more to it than that." I don't know how I'm so certain about this, but I am.

"Yes." Rustle lands beside me. "I also went because normally, I'm so strong. It's the others who are sick. If they see me hurt, it just makes things worse for everyone."

"So you didn't want to frighten them."

"Yes, and there was enough to scare everybody that day. Didn't the clouds frighten you?"

"What do you mean?"

"When the sky turned purple. It happened the night before we met."

"I slept pretty soundly that night. If the clouds changed color, I wouldn't have noticed anything."

Rustle's wings slump. "Oh."

"Why don't you tell me what it means to be the sacrifice? I can tell that you want to."

"Not yet." Rustle twists her hands by her waistline. "Maybe tomorrow." Rustle takes to the skies again. "We should make camp. It's very late."

We stopped at rolling meadow. Rustle flits around for a bit before waving her arms. Purple sparkles tumble from her hands. Where the violet particles touch the ground, a pair of willow trees rise from the earth. The many branches weave together into a pair of very comfy-looking nests.

I step closer to the bigger of the two. "Is this for me?"

"It is." Rustle flits nearby. Her eyes are wide with worry.

I scan the structure carefully. Sprigs of lavender line the bottom. "It's a beautiful bed, Rustle. I'm sure I'll sleep very well here."

Rustle beams. "Glad you like it." She settles into her smaller bed. The lilac flowers grow over her to create a blanket. "I'll take you to the Sentinel tomorrow."

"Thank you." In celebration, my tail does its version of a happy dance. I shake my hips in a half-hearted attempt to join in, but I don't get too far.

All of a sudden, I can't remember being more tired. I crawl into my own bed and promptly fall asleep.

30

LINCOLN

That night, I don't dream. Pounding drums keep interrupting my rest. Every time they strike up, I pull the broken silencer ring off my thumb and slip on a fresh one.

By the time morning rolls around, I don't feel like I've slept much at all. It doesn't help that I awaken to find Kell standing in my doorway. The moment I notice him, my silencer ring shimmies on my thumb. There's no need for me to look down. I already know what just happened.

That was my last silencer ring and it cracked. Where once was quiet, now the low thud of drums fills my head.

I sit up. "What is it, Kell?"

He marches closer and inspects me carefully. "What's your name?"

No question what the ringmaster is up to. I've seen other warriors around here. All of them use their stage name. Some even sport their costumes twenty-four/seven. When Kell asks their name, they probably don't even remember what it was before the arena.

When I speak, it is in a loud and steady voice. "I am Lincoln Vidar Osric Aquilus, King of the Thrax and Consort to the Great Scala."

Those are just the words I say. But the tone I use carries a very different meaning: *Fuck you, Kell.*

"I've seen the little trinkets you use against my magic," says Kell. "Those rings won't work forever."

"I appreciate your concern over my welfare." Leaning forward, I rest my elbows on my knees. "Let's see. Our deal was for how many fights again?"

Kell glares at me. I'm happy to note how his body positively vibrates with rage. The tiny glass vials along his utility belt softly jangle against each other.

With that, I know one thing. I'm winning. Since that's one of my favorite things to do, it puts me in a rather jovial mood, despite the low thud of drums.

I count off the battles on my fingers. "First, I took on the ratatoskr. Second, the jotnar. That leaves two more.

Tonight, tomorrow and then? You must end your bargain with Connor." Reaching into my pocket, I pull out the runestone. "Still have it." I then check the back of my hand. The blue hammer shimmers with magic. "And I've this as well. It seems our deal remains in place."

Kell folds his arms over his chest. "You're strong. That's all to my plan. I'm a creator. A master. I can't fashion good games without the right raw materials. When you break—and that will happen—then I'll have the perfect tool for my purposes."

"Good to know. If you don't mind, I must get ready for my day."

Kell steps out the door and pauses. Little by little, he swings around to face me again. "What are you really working at? There must be some plan. You can't possibly think my magic won't break you down before the fourth game."

Cold swirls within me and it has nothing to do with the magic all around. This is exactly what Myla and I wanted to avoid. We can't have Kell suspecting our true scheme.

Kell moves closer. "You didn't answer my question before. Have you been to Lower Gurith?"

"Why would I go there?"

I've seen hounds when they catch a scent. Their ears perk up while their eyes take on a dark light. That's the precise expression that Kell wears now. "You'd visit because your mother is from the House of Gurith. They're Viking thrax. Do you really think I wouldn't know about them?"

"I appreciate your interest in my lineage. I suppose I might have stepped through Lower Gurith at some point. It's a large realm and I have many duties."

"Ever heard of Underland? It's connected to Lower Gurith."

I can see where this interrogation is going, and it's a place that's far too close to Myla for my liking.

"Don't bother lying." Kell rests his hand on the skull which hangs from his belt. "I can find things out myself easily enough."

Clearly, that skull is some kind of magic totem. If Kell consults it, then this entire plan could go sideways. I must get him derailed.

I force a sigh. "That's an excellent idea. Seek out every place where I've done a royal visit. Spend the day casting spells somewhere that is *not here.* I've important things of my own to do." Rising, I go over to my backpack and sift through the contents.

All the while, anxiety spikes through my nervous system. What if Kell takes me up on my suggestion? If he casts spells, then Myla and I are in deep trouble.

Kell marches toward the door.

One step.

Two.

My heart beats with such force, I can feel my pulse in my throat.

Three.

Then Kell stops once more. Some of the worry seeps from my bones. Kell is taking the bait.

"What's in that pack?" asks the ringmaster.

"Nothing. I need to get ready. Surely, you do that in the mornings." I quickly zip up the bag. Turning, I hold the item behind my back.

There, that should look mighty suspicious.

Kell lifts his arm. With slow movements, he examines the blue mark I set on the back of his hand. "You can cast spells, too. Don't think I've forgotten."

"Why are you still here?"

Kell's smirk returns. "You know, we never did finish our tour yesterday. There's an entire wing that's deserted. It's where you and your family will live when you fail your side of our arrangement."

Yes. I'd much rather another day of meandering around with Kell. As long as I can keep an eye on him, I know the ringmaster isn't tracking down Myla.

I take care to slump my shoulders. "I'm not sure."

"What? Don't tell me the King of Thrax is afraid of another little tour."

"I fear nothing," I say smoothly.

And now that I know I can keep Kell away from Myla? Those words are actually true.

31

LINCOLN

*H*ours pass as Kell leads me through a series of empty chambers. It's clear families once lived here, perhaps back when the arena was more popular... and there were more warriors. But now? Everything is coated in a thin layer of dust.

The ringmaster makes a point of showing me where we'll put Maxon's crib. It takes a supreme effort not to throttle him where he stands.

The tour goes on. We see swimming pools and training ranges. There are storage halls and hidden passageways. All in all, it reminds me of an evil version of Antrum.

It's in one of the portrait halls that Kell makes his mistake. We pause before a massive painting of the god Vidarr slaying the beast Fenrir.

"See that?" asks Kell. "The beast Fenrir killed Vidarr's father, Odin. In turn, Vidarr slays the monster."

"You once said your culture is all about the debt of sons to fathers."

"So it is."

"Remember all those years ago on demon patrol? You killed the baby demon because its father was dead. If you really followed the story of Vidarr, then the child would have lived and served up vengeance."

"No." Kell's eyes flash. "You're wrong."

I haven't spent my life reading reactions not to know what's happening now. I've found a weak spot in Kell's thinking.

Best to push.

"I've studied the Norse Universe," I continue. I can't think of a single instance of a son being killed because the father had died young."

The pounding of the drums grows louder. Kell bares his teeth. "Why don't you just give in?"

"Perhaps your magic isn't strong enough to break me. You spend so much time trying to make everything perfect. What are you trying to hide?"

Kell's mouth slowly winds into a smile. "Only that it's time for you to fight again. We've spent all day together and yet, you've only felt as if a few hours have passed." He steps closer. "Does that surprise you?"

"It did when you first pulled that trick," I reply. "Not now."

The muscles of Kell's throat tighten. "You won't live through this fight."

I smile. "And you won't hide your secrets much longer."

The sand beneath my feet churns. Kell stares at me, dumbfounded, as I get pulled under for my third battle.

32

LINCOLN

*M*oments later, I resurface on the arena. Giant Kell looms nearby.

"Tonight, we offer you a new spectacle of warrior prowess with Baculum!"

The crowd cheers. Drumbeats swell. The projected version of the ringmaster vanishes.

Huh. That's a new one.

Normally, Kell drags out this part of the games. At a bare minimum, the ringmaster announces what kind of monster I'm about to fight.

All in all, there's only one reason Kell's keeping my opponent a secret. He wants to preserve the element of surprise.

At this point, I have to hand it to Kell. The guy does not give up. No matter how badly I kick his puppet-fighters in any one battle, he regroups and comes back. Whatever this mystery foe might be, it's definitely a new strategy to win.

Honestly, if Kell wasn't an evil elf from another dimension, he'd be perfect for demon patrol.

A slower drumbeat fills the arena. The audience claps in rhythm. I take out my baculum and stare into the darkness at the other side of the arena floor.

Something will soon step out from those shadows. But what?

A figure marches onto the floor. My breath catches. It's Connor. His face is wild with rage as he ignites his own baculum into a longbow and shoots fiery arrows in my direction.

The crowd turns shrill with delight. My head gets woozy. After what he pulled with Maxon, my father isn't exactly winning any Dad Of The Year awards.

But he wouldn't attack me in the arena, right?

I leap aside just as the blazing arrows impact the nearby sand. *That was close.* Father or not, I must get my head in this battle.

Footsteps sound behind me. Twisting around, I see Connor racing toward me in full body armor. His baculum longsword is held high above his head, ready to strike.

But that can't be. Father was just half-way across the arena. How did he get over here so quickly?

An awareness dawns. Suddenly, I know exactly what kind of monster I'm up against. A mare. These creatures take the form of your worst nightmare.

Fake Connor rushes closer. Igniting my own baculum into a longsword, I meet his strike with my blade. Our weapons slam with such force, Fake Connor's baculum gets knocked from his grip.

That won't happen twice. Kell is puppeteering this mare. No doubt, the ringmaster has noticed how his last hit didn't carry enough power. Next time, Fake Connor will push much harder.

For a moment, I can see the mare as it really is: a skeletal creature with leathery skin and pointed ears. It stares at its hand in disbelief, not sure how its sword got knocked away.

Sadly, it isn't the only one who's having issues adjusting to what's happening. In a flash, the mare retakes Connor's shape. My first instinct is to run. How can I raise my sword against my father?

Then I recall the truth. This battle is an illusion. What's real is how Myla is out there fighting for me and Maxon.

I simply must give her more time.

Straightening my shoulders, I reignite my baculum.

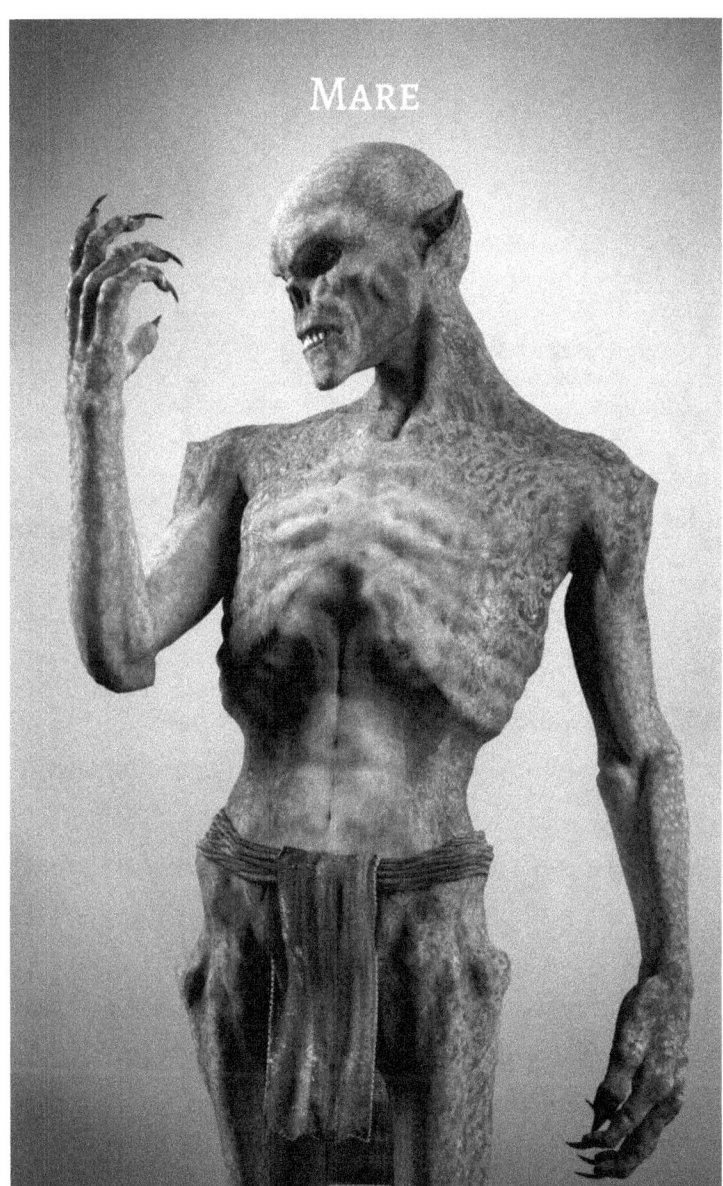

MARE

LINCOLN

I firm up my battle stance. Fake Connor rounds on me. This time, he tries a new tactic. The false version of my father holds his arms wide, showing how he's not attacking.

"I only want to protect you and your family."

Fake Connor steps closer. The drumming grows louder.

"Don't you remember how I first placed a wooden sword in your hand? How can you doubt my heart?"

Ten feet away.

I grip my baculum but don't ignite them. Somehow, it's just not possible.

"You're my only son. You know I love you."

Five feet.

"What would Octavia think if she saw this?

Two feet.

Kell's voice sounds in my head.

"Light your baculum."

"Swipe right."

"Take him down."

With every order, it's harder to hold my ground and not become Kell's puppet.

Fake Connor pauses right before me. "You've always been mine to use. Never forget that. And Maxon is next." He ignites his baculum as a dagger and goes to stab me through the heart. It's a reflex to raise my arm and block the blow. The blade slices through my body armor and nicks my forearm. Blood sprays across my chest.

It's the sight of my own blood that does it. I snap out of my haze, ignite my baculum as a longsword, and lift the blade high.

Then I strike.

Only I don't hit the mare with the sharp side of the blade. Instead, I slam the creature's head with the baculum rods themselves. The impact is sudden and fierce.

Fake Connor falls over, unconscious.

My legs feel liquid beneath me. I can't believe it. I

almost listened to those orders from Kell. Shaking my head, I stalk off the arena floor. One question bites at my soul.

How much longer can I hold out here?

LINCOLN

I march off the arena floor and through an exit archway. Once again, a lone figure awaits me in the darkened passage.

Walker.

"That fight was…" Walker shakes his head.

"A disaster," I finish. "I'm aware. Did you find any more silencer rings?"

"Not yet." Walker takes a half-step backward. "You already went through all the others I found?"

"They barely lasted the night."

Walker looks around the empty passage. "What kind of magic is behind this place?"

"You have no idea."

Walker slowly scans me from head to toe. I know what he sees. Blood spatters on my body armor. Dark circles under my eyes. Deathly pale skin. And my external appearance doesn't compare to the mess inside my head. The constant drumming makes me want to puncture both of my inner ears.

"Lincoln, I've known you all your life. Every man has his limits. Listen to me carefully. You've found yours."

"Yet I'm still vertical."

"You almost killed that creature. It was begging for mercy and still, you almost drove you baculum through its throat. These games are changing you."

At those words, the power of the arena presses into me harder than ever before. Ice seems to run through my veins. Walker is speaking the truth. So why can't I just leave this place? Xavier and Camilla would love to start a war for my son. Octavia would ensure this arena is wiped clean from the Dark Lands. Why not set this burden down?

Walker clasps my shoulders. "You think you're helping Myla and Maxon, but what if while you're trying to make everything perfect for them, you're just turning yourself into someone they won't even know?" He lowers his voice. "This is what happened to Connor."

"What?" My voice comes out rough. "How do you know?"

"I've been alive for a long time. Your father always wanted to be the ideal parent and king. I don't know what choices he made along the way, but I can tell you this. Connor wanted perfection and it destroyed him."

Bands of sorrow tighten around my chest. "I can't listen to this now, Walker."

"But you mist. The way your father lives? That's the way Kell acts as well. The ringmaster wants the Viking Games to be flawless. It tries to control everything. But no matter what Kell does, it's never enough."

I rub my neck. All the while, the drums thuds louder, making it even harder to focus. Even so, the facts here are clear. "And if I turn my troubles over? They'll bring in armies. Didn't your people do that when Kell first arrived?"

"That's not important."

"What happened when Kell first arrived? Don't tell me you don't know."

Walker slumps his shoulders. "My people sent in an army of demons and ghouls to face down Kell. Everyone burned up before they even reached the Arena floor. No survivors. The light elves only escaped when some thrax faced off with Kell in direct combat. It gave the light elves a chance to cast their own spells."

I meet Walker's gaze. "I love you, my friend. And I can leave now, but we both know I'll just end up with worse problems. This is the plan Myla and I created together. I know she's out there, somewhere, making it happen. I'm holding on."

Walker doesn't speak. An ink-black tear rolls down his cheek. The sight makes the cold bite even more deeply inside me. But there's nothing I can do right now, either for myself or Walker.

Turning away, I begin the long trek back to my cell.

Myla, I'm won't give up on you and Maxon.

MYLA

*L*et the record show that if light elves ever want to make a killing in retail, they should package up these willow tree beds. I can't remember the last time I slept this well.

For her part, Rustle wakes up super-early. She spends the morning chattering away about what it's like to be an envy elf.

Spoiler alert: it's a lot like being an envy quasi.

Even so, this is much better than all the offers of mushroom bits, so I play along. I speed through breakfast and getting ready.

On a similar note, if the thrax ever want to kick ass in retail, they could sell their handi-wipe charms. Just touch one of these puppies to whatever you want cleansed. There's a burst of blue light and—WHAMMO —you're hygienic as fuck.

It's not as pleasant as a hot shower, but I'm stuck in an enchanted world with a strange elf. It doesn't do to be picky.

As we march along, the open meadows become dotted with thin trees. Soon the trunks grow thicker, the branches taller, and the leaves wider. In no time, an imposing forest towers around us.

Rustle and I walk under the darkened canopy.

"We're nearly at the village," says Rustle. "The Sentinel will be here."

"Good new—"

I pause. My tail arcs over my shoulder.

Someone watches.

My skin prickles over with awareness. I step around in a slow circle. As my eyes adjust to the shadows, I can see them. Light elves stand in the trees.

And damn, do they ever look like crap.

LIGHT ELVES

MYLA

For a moment, I'm at a total loss. With a name like *light elves*, you'd think they'd be all sunshine and smiles. These folks look neither happy nor healthy. If I had to guess, life in Antrum doesn't agree with them. Which I totally understand. Living under ghoul rule didn't float my personal boat either.

The trees gently shake as more elves step out. Hundreds watch me and Rustle walk by. After a short march, we step into a wide clearing. The Sentinel kneels in the center of the grassy space. An elf child sits in her lap.

The Sentinel sways from side to side. "No need to cry, Blossom. Your mother will be home soon."

This sight stops me in my tracks. When I'd pictured

this moment, I planned to rip into the Sentinel for leaving me at the temple.

Now? I'm not so sure.

Maybe it's my new maternal status, but there's no missing the gentle way the Sentinel cuddles this little girl. Other elves keep approach the pair and offer to take Blossom away. The child only burrows her head against the Sentinel and refuses to move.

I step over to Rustle. "When the Sentinel left the temple, she went to see Blossom, didn't she?"

Rustle nods. "Poor Blossom. Her dad was a sacrifice like me. Only he didn't make it."

Now, I haven't been pushing the whole sacrifice thing with Rustle lately. It seemed like she'd blab when she was ready. Maybe if I ask now, I'll get an actual answer.

"So what's this sacrifice thing all about?" I ask.

Thunder rumbles across the sky. Blossom leaps up and reaches toward the clouds. "Mommy! Mommy!"

"Want to know what a sacrifice is?" asks Rustle. "See for yourself."

Deep violet mists roll across the sky. Shadows deepen all around. Another peal of thunder booms through the air. Lightning bursts within the swirling clouds.

The purple mists swirl above us. Blossom jumps

toward the skies, her petite features tight with worry. The center of the spinning cloud slowly lowers toward the ground, tornado-style. Wind roars in my ears. Leaves rip free from the trees. Branches break loose.

The tornado touches the ground near Blossom. More lightning flashes inside the cloudy depths. Another deep roll of thunder sounds. The cone of cloud rises back up into the sky. The mists fade. Shadows vanish.

A new figure now stands in the clearing and it's a freaking nightmare. And by this I mean, that it's a Mare, a Norse monster that fights by inducing horrible visions in their victims. The creature a skeletal thing with leathery green skin and pointy ears.

My tail arches over my shoulder, ready to fight. I pull out my baculum from their holster. There is no way I am allowing this monster to cause trouble.

I may be concerned, but none of the elves seem worried. For her part, Blossom clutches at the Mare's legs.

Purple sand bubbles around the Mare's feet. The particles crawl up the monster, covering it in a thick layer of sand. When the violet coating recedes, there's no Mare any more.

It's a tiny lady elf. The woman scoops Blossom into her arms. "Mommy's back," she cries.

The Sentinel watches the scene with a smile. Other elves come forward to encircle Blossom and her mother. Folks press their palms against her wings and shoulders.

I set my hand on my throat. "When you're the sacrifice, it means you allow Kell top pull you into the Viking Games." I look to Rustle. "The Norse monsters don't come from another universe. The ringmaster drags you in and changes your appearance. No wonder he has to puppeteer your every move. None of you are warriors."

Rustle nods. "Only chooses the strongest of us to become sacrifices."

"Does the Sentinel fight?"

Rustle sniffs. "We won't let her. Only wrath elves can rule our kind. She's the last one."

My heart sinks. "That must be lonely."

"Not for much longer, though." Rustle smiles. "Soon you'll get us a golden apple. We'll make the wish to go home."

I smile. "That's the plan." An idea hits me. "When you were the sacrifice, what monster did you become?"

"I was a ratatoskr."

I lift my brows. "A humanoid rodent? Whoa. What was the fight like?"

"When I started off, I was fighting two thrax. Well, I wasn't really doing anything. All I could hear are these drums. And I felt Kell inside my head, making me kick and swipe."

"And one of those thrax hurt your foot?"

"No, not those two. Kell sent them away. Another thrax came onto the arena floor. It was just me and that thrax."

I frown. "I thought it was always one monster against two thrax?"

"As a rule, but not with Baculum."

"What did you say the name was?"

"Baculum. He used a fire sword in battle and could have killed me. Throughout the fight, I still felt Kell in my head, only now the ringmaster was angry. He was only controlling my half of the battle. Baculum was too strong for Kell to control. I think he was supposed to kill me, but he threw me against a wall instead. That's how I hurt my foot."

I can't help but grin. "I think I know who you fought. Baculum must be my husband, Lincoln. He went to the games to try and distract Kell."

Rustle sighs. "That's too bad."

My heart sinks. "Why?"

"I'm from the Norse Universe. Kell can take over my mind, but it's not permanent." She shakes her head. "It's not that way for people from this reality."

My insides twist with worry. "How long do the warriors last against Kell?"

"I've fought in the arena six times," says Rustle. "I've never seen a fighter resist Kell for more than a few minutes."

I gasp. "Lincoln's been fighting for three days."

"Oh," says Rustle. Her eyes widen with sympathy.

I step closer. "Once Lincoln leaves the arena, he'll be back to normal, right? I mean, Kell doesn't actually turn their minds into mush forever, right?"

Rustle stares at he ground. "I'm so sorry."

I march over to the Sentinel. "Hey, remember me?"

"I do. Sorry for running off, but Blossom was frantic. I could hear her cries across Underland. I didn't know when you'd be back… but I did figured you'd find me quickly enough."

"I did. And now, I'm ready to get those golden apples."

"You're right. Let's move out."

We march through the night. All the other light elves follow us. I can't help but ask a few times if we can magically transport around Underland. That would be a big *no.*

My world becomes a blur of trees, mist and muscle ache. But every time I'm tempted to stop, my conversation with Rustle rings through my head.

I've never had a fighter resist Kell for more than a few minutes.

It seems to take forever, but eventually we reach another open field. At last, the Sentinel stops.

"We're here," she announces.

"And where is the tree?"

The Sentinel shrugs. "I've only seen it appear once. That was right after we first came to this place."

"I got that part. But I got the impression that the tree was back. I mean, I've got a husband who's being brainwashed by an evil elf here. What if Idunn doesn't bring back her tree?"

The Sentinel lifts her chin. "The tree will rise again."

I force out as long breath. "Okay, I got that." I jog in place. "We can make this happen."

Come on, Idunn.

LINCOLN

I don't remember returning to my cell.

Or falling asleep.

But I do recall my dreams. I'm back in the Viking Games and fighting the Mare again. Kell's voice keeps echoing in my brain, along with the heavy pounding of drums.

"Light your baculum."

"Swipe right."

"Jump now."

Each demand ricochets through my nervous system. It takes everything in me not to do as ordered.

Somehow, I know if I give in, I'll forget being Lincoln. I won't let that happen.

When I awaken, I'm exhausted. I force down the last

of my food from my backpack. Every muscle in my body feels strained. And my mind is almost hollowed out.

I check my watch and my heart cracks.

It's almost 8 p.m.

Sure enough, the floor of my cell transforms into purple sand. The particles bubble and rise up my legs. I've been through this before. No question what this means.

Time to fight again.

38

MYLA

I pace around the open meadow. Minutes tick by and there's no sign of any tree. A hundred light elves wait at the outskirts of the clearing.

The Sentinel steps to my side. "Are you sure you want to do this?"

"Hell, yes. If the tree shows up, I'll get two apples. One for you and one for me."

The Sentinel sets her hand on my shoulder. "That's not what I meant. What if nothing appears?"

My stomach tumbles. "The tree should have showed up by now, right?"

"I'm afraid so."

"Okay, fine." I crack my neck. "I'm a goddess. Sort of. Idunn's got some powers. We can talk." I cup my hand by my mouth. "Idunn! It's Mya Lewis here. I've been a queen for a short time, but I've been a warrior almost all my life. And I have some supernatural powers. Here's the deal. I need some golden apples from your tree to save my husband and son." I press my palm against my stomach. "You care a lot about pregnant women and warriors. I need your help."

I pause, wait and watch. So do all the very pathetic-looking little elves.

Nothing happens.

Maybe it's my pregnancy hormones, but the silence makes me lose my ever-loving mind. I pull out my baculum from their holster on my spine and ignite them into a single spear made from white flame. I slam the weapon into the ground. It meets the purple earth with a low hiss.

"Listen to me, honey. All I want are two apples to save my family… and to bring my friends here back to their home. You've got a whole tree of these things. So either cough up some wood or believe me, I will use my powers on your ass. Once I'm dead, I'll igni myself into outer space and haunt you for eternity. Think this little speech is annoying? Wait until I'm following you around forever. You hear me?"

No reply.

All of a sudden, the ground rumbles. Amber clouds

roll across the skies. A yellow hue permeates the land-scape. Before me, the earth breaks apart.

A great golden tree raises up and spreads its branches. The thing is lousy with golden apples.

Yes.

GOLDEN APPLES OF IDUNN

39

MYLA

*N*ow that's a beautiful sight. *The Golden Apples of Idunn.* Sadly, I'm not the only one who thinks so. The light elves swarm around the tree. Some dance. Others sing.

Most try to climb.

They don't get more than a few feet up the trunk before the entire tree shimmies. Small arcs of power zap into the light elves, sending them tumbling to the ground.

Okay, that doesn't look pleasant.

Still, who cares? This is for Lincoln and Maxon.

Cracking my neck, I step up to the towering tree. Fortunately, this is one of the many situations where having a tail is the bomb. Bracing myself, I grip the trunk, waiting for the shock of power to send me onto my ass.

That doesn't happen.

My fingers actually sink into the bark. I quickly scale up and out onto a heavy branch. With my tail as an anchor, I swing up to stand. The arbor is dotted with tons of apples. I scope out some of the closest. I pick two that are about the size of my fist and pluck them.

The fruit is smooth, cold and beautiful. I catch my own reflection in the glistening surface. In this moment, I can't remember seeing anything more lovely.

Two apples.

Two wishes.

This nightmare is so close to being over.

Far below me, the light elves cheer. The Sentinel breaks out into a song of celebration. Some elves take to the skies and dance. The moment seems frozen in gold, just like the apples themselves.

Smiling, I hold the fruit against my chest with my left hand. Using my right arm and tail, I start climbing down the trunk.

That's when the tree goes berserk. The entire arbor wobbles. Tiny arcs of power shift and arc across the bark. All the branches reach toward me at once and twist around my body, mummy style. Soon I'm wrapped up from head to toe.

The world turns dark.

The sensation of being confined transforms into one of floating in infinite space. I'm suspended in star-filled eternity. Cold bites into my skin.

And a big ass goddess stands above me. She's lovely, pale and dressed in leather. A metal headdress glistens atop her head. She grips a tall staff in her right hand.

"I am the goddess Idunn," she says, her voice booming across the infinite space.

Huh. This can't be good.

IDUNN

40

MYLA

So that certainly looks like a goddess. And this is definitely some kind of spell. Because no one just floats in outer space without oxygen and whatnot.

I give her what I hope is friendly wave. "Hey, there. I'm Myla."

"How dare you threaten me, you lowly creature?"

I sniff. "If you think I'm backing off the haunting thing, you can forget it." I clutch the apples more tightly against my chest. "I'm taking these apples and that's it."

"You wish my bounty," says Idunn. "Therefore, you must prove worth."

I frown. "As in, right now?

Idunn flashes me a look that says, *I won't ask you again.*

"Ooooookay."

Think fast, Myla.

An idea appears.

"I shall prove worth with a story. How does that work for you?"

Idunn just glares at me in reply, so I take that as a *yes*.

"Once upon a time, there was a beautiful future momma who hauled her ass underground and through a magic forest, all in search of two measly pieces of fruit. She got the apples, but then a goddess yanked her out into outer space and asked for proof that she deserved the apples. But once the goddess realized how hard it was to get to this very point in the story, she stopped being a bitch with a tinfoil hat and just let our heroine take her shit and go."

I was doing pretty well until I got to the bitch part. But I'm hoping that Idunn looks past all that.

The goddess narrows her eyes. "I shall give you one chance to prove worth."

The next thing I know, I'm tumbling down through outer space. Light flashes around me. An ethereal wind whips through my hair. I sense branches around me again. Then they're gone and I'm free falling over the wide landscape of Underland.

I land on my ass with a thud.

All the elves stand around me, their eyes wide and mouths open. The Sentinel steps forward.

"What happened?" she asks.

"I had a little chat with Idunn and she let me keep two apples." I angle my hand to show off my bounty.

Aaaaaaaaad there's only one apple.

The Sentient frowns. "What happened? We all saw you pluck two apples."

"Well, I did. Then Idunn magicked me off into outer space and took one of them."

The Sentient steps closer. "Why would Idunn do that?"

"She said something about giving proof. As instructions go, it was totally sketchy pants."

"The tree is still here," says the Sentinel. "Just climb up and get one more."

"Sure thing."

The ground rumbles and splits open. Wind whips around us. The golden tree shakes and crumples into the earth. The clearing turns quiet. Moments ago, the elves were flying, singing and dancing. Now, they all stare at the Sentinel. A sense of despair hangs around us, heavy as rain.

"You only have one apple," says the Sentinel. "Use it to save your family."

I clutch the fruit against my chest. "You're sure?"

The Sentinel nods. "I won't save my people at the expense of yours."

I lift the fruit and open my mouth. But I can't take a bite.

"Look," I begin. "I know what it's like to be forced to serve someone against your will. I can't leave you guys like this."

Suddenly, purple clouds roll across the sky, then begin to swirl. Thunder booms. Small bolts of lightning spark in the depths.

The Sentinel sighs. "That is the sign. I must now choose our next sacrifice. It is time for you to leave us." She takes a step back. "Bite the apple. Make your wish. Go."

My eyes widen. Another idea appears.

"You need a sacrifice?" I ask. "I'll do it."

"But you can't. You're not from the Norse Universe."

I toss the apple between my palms. "Fortunately, I know an easy way to fix that." Lifting the fruit to my mouth, I bite down hard and make my wish.

I want to be the next sacrifice.

With that, everything changes.

LINCOLN

The purple sand pulls me under. I don't how long I stay there. At some point, I rise up again. Light burns into my eyes. Particles lower from my body.

I stand in the center of the Viking Arena.

Giant Kell looms above me. "And now, for tonight's main event... another fight with Baculum!"

The crowd roars. Fresh drum beats sound. The audience claps in time with the rhythm.

My thoughts blur. I can't tell if I'm asleep or awake.

Kell's voice sounds inside my head. *"Ignite your baculum,"* he orders. *"Wave to the crowd."*

The urge to pull my baculum from their holster turns intense. I ball my hands into fists and stand in place.

I can't give in.

Giant Kell speaks again. "This marks the forth fight for Baculum to battle in the Viking Games. Are you ready to see the monster that will face him?"

The audience cheers so loud, the sound makes my bones vibrate.

"Behold!" cries Giant Kell. "A new creature arrives from the Norse Universe!"

Kell's voice sounds in my head once more. *"Give in. Be my instrument. We're a lot alike. You travel to Earth and fight demons. I went to another realm in search of my fortune. We'll be stronger together, I promise. Just ignite your baculum."*

I hold my ground. "No. What are you hiding?" The truth hits me. All the hints about sacrifice and fathers. "You have a son, don't you? What did you do to him?"

"You don't understand. I has to made the ultimate sacrifice. My son was a better mage than I'll ever be. I needed his magic to reach this reality, so I killed him. Do you know how hard that was to do? I've had to sacrifice so much to make these games. Now they must be perfect in his honor. Ignite!"

"No. Your mistakes are your own. How you must have rejoiced when Father agreed to sacrifice his grandson, just as you offered up your own child. But I won't do the same with Maxon. Begin this fight and I will win." I raise my fist, showing off the blue mark on the back of my hand. "This is the symbol of your vow. I already fought the ratatoskr, jotnar and mare. Send me any Norse monster and I'll end them. Then you'll have to make good on your word."

"There is one monster you'll never defeat," whispers Kell in my mind. *"And that's one who fights with magic."*

High above the arena floor, Giant Kell calls out to the crowd. "Tonight, Baculum will fight a different kind of foe. Me."

Next Giant Kell does something I didn't know was possible. He turns solid. I'd always thought of the giant version of Kell as a projection. But this is something different. I'm now facing off with a giant.

Good thing I've done that once already.

Giant Kell now takes the skull from his belt. After it's removed, it swells to the size of a helmet.

Once more, Kell's voice sounds in my mind. *"This is my son's skull. His life was never his own. Neither is yours. Your father gave it to me... along with that of your wife and child."*

The massive version of Kell sets the new helm atop his head.

Then he transforms.

Kell's massive body bursts with flame. Raising his voice, the ringmaster takes the vow.

I commit my life to the Viking Games!

Like so many others before him, a blue mark now glows on Kell's skin. It's the image of a longsword. With a burst of flame, the same weapon appears in his right hand. Kell raises the blade high. This is the same movement he'd been wanting me to do and with good reason.

The crowd cheers louder and longer than I ever thought possible.

KELL

42

LINCOLN

iery Kell keeps his sword raised high. Drumbeats swell. The crowd cheers itself hoarse. From the corner of my eye, I spot a figure standing in one of the access archways.

Walker.

With Fiery Kell whipping the crowd into a frenzy, no one cares if I jog a few yards over to the arch.

Walker's eyes are wide with worry. "You can't fight that thing." Walker gestures toward Fiery Kell. "Let me help you."

There's no question what reply Walker expects here. He thinks I'll ask him to open a ghoul portal and transport us both away.

That's not an option.

"You still have the Aquilineans in the audience?"

"Yes." Walker's brows pull together in a look of confusion. "I can open a portal for you. We don't need them."

"Tell your people to clear everyone out. Things are about to get toasty."

Walker does a double-take. "You're not leaving?"

"No, the audience is."

"Don't ask me to do this. I can't abandon you here."

"You're clearing out the spectators as well as yourself. That's an order from your king."

"I refuse."

I pull off my own helmet and toss it aside. "Then do it as my friend. Please."

"All right." Walker forces a smile. "If anyone can make this happen, it's you. Keep fighting, Lincoln." He steps back into the shadows. I turn to face the battle ahead.

It's true that I've always been *fortune's favorite.* Yet at some point, everyone's luck runs out.

Perhaps my time has come.

43

MYLA

I bite down into the sweetest apple ever. Around me, all the elves stare. Fear and awe are etched into their lovely faces. I swallow the sweet mouthful and speak the words aloud.

"I want to be the next sacrifice."

The apple glows with golden light. That same brightness leeches over onto my hand, up my arm, and over every inch of my body. Foreign magic churns within my soul.

I change.

My ears turn pointy. Wings sprout up my back. My fighting suit becomes a skimpy yellow gown.

The Sentinel gasps. "You're one of us now."

"Good," I declare. Purple clouds churn overhead.

Leaning back on my heels, I reach toward the sky with both arms. "Come and get me."

The purple clouds swirl into a violent tornado. Winds whip around the clearing. All the elves cuddle against the ground so they don't get swept away.

Little by little, the tornado dips down toward me.

Then it stops.

I look to the Sentinel. "What's happening?"

She closes her eyes. "It's Kell. He's changed his mind. He's going to be tonight's Norse monster. We don't need to send a sacrifice."

Oh, no.

44

LINCOLN

iery Kell swipes his longsword at me. The blade itself is about five times my height. With one strike, I could be cut in two.

But I know the ringmaster. He wants to drag out the battle and please his audience.

Instead of slicing me apart, Fiery Kell swats me with the flat side of the blade. The weapon strikes my head and sends me flying across the arena floor. I slide right into the same access archway where I just spoke with Walker.

My vision blurs. A new figure stands under the arch, but my brain's too fuzzy to catch details.

"Walker, is that you?"

"No, it's me."

My heart sinks. Connor is here.

I shake my head and try to stop my vision from spinning. *Doesn't help.*

"I'm busy," I state. "Not sure if you noticed."

"I've been watching the games for a while now. I was afraid Baculum was you. Once you took off your helmet, I knew for certain." He kneels beside me. "What have I done?"

I force myself to stand. It isn't easy. And once I'm upright, the best I can do is sway like a drunkard.

"I brought you a transport charm." Connor offers me a ring. "You can get out of here. All Kell wants is Maxon. You don't need to lose your life over this."

Somehow, I'm able to fix Father with an icy glare. "What I said before is even more true. My son is his own person. He's not some extension of my will... or yours."

"Is that what you really want?"

"Exactly."

"Then I won't be involved."

I stifle a groan. "Those are our choices—you take total control or vanish from my child's life?"

"I'm only trying to do what's best. You need to trust me."

"No, *you* need to leave. If that means you aren't part of Maxon's future, then it's your loss. For now, just back the Hell off and let me handle this."

Without waiting for another word from Father, I turn and stride into the battle.

45

MYLA

The Sentinel takes my hands in hers. "Don't worry. You can be the sacrifice next time."

"You don't understand. Most warriors don't last five minutes against Kell. Rustle told me herself. I can't wait. There might not be any next time."

The Sentinel tilts her head. "What would you have us do?"

"You guys have your own magic. Rustle used it to make beds when we were camping. Now shoot that power toward the purple clouds and get my ass out of here."

"My people are already weak. We already let you have the golden apple. Why should we do this as well?"

"Because once I get to the arena, I will destroy Kell. That might not send you back to your home world, but at least you won't be forced to fight in his games anymore. That's got to mean something."

The Sentinel hugs her elbows. "I'm not sure if we can even combine magic that way. We only work to use our powers alone."

Rustle steps up. "But we don't know it *won't* work, right?"

"Thank you, girlfriend." We share a fist bump.

I turn to the other elves in the clearing. "You guys want to leave this world, and I most definitely want to save my son and husband. So let's give this a try. Envy elves, I need you to think about my backpack. I know you've all been eyeing it since we left the village. Work that jealous mojo. Pride elves, picture how pretty you are. And wrath elves—or rather elf—contemplate how awesome it would be to kick Kell's butt."

"You've been trapped in here for hundreds of years," I continue. "My people were stuck once, too. Then I leveraged some lightning bolts and kicked our so-called overlords out of town. You can do the same thing. Everyone has some magic. Focus on the count of three. 1, 2, 3!"

Before when Rustle created our willow bed, a thin dusting of purple sparkles had tumbled from her hands. Now a column of the stuff rises from each elf. All their powers combine into a swirling geyser of magic that shoots straight up into the sky.

There's still some purple magic remaining in the clouds. Now that power gets linked to the column of energy from the ground.

No question what to do next.

I step right into the combined pillar of violet magic. Energy whips around me. Every bone in my body seems to shimmy. Bright purple light burns into my eyes.

One moment, I'm in Underland.

The next, I'm on the floor of the Viking Arena.

At last.

46

LINCOLN

I walk away from my father and toward Ringmaster Kell. The world takes on a dreamlike sheen. Drums pound so loudly, my head feels as if it's splitting in two.

Fiery Kell towers above me. He raises his massive sword. This time, the cutting edge is angled toward my throat.

It's all too much. The drums. My father. Ringmaster Kell. In this moment, it's all I can do to stand in place and take death without flinching.

Fiery Kell begins to lower his sword.

"Lincoln!"

Every nerve ending in my body goes on alert. *That sounds like Myla.* Just hearing her voice makes me swing into action. I leap away from Kell's blow. The massive sword impacts the arena floor with a spray of sand.

"Back off, Smokey. That's my husband."

My heart soars. *Back off, Smokey?* That's definitely Myla.

I jump to my feet and turn around. There she is: my wife and angelbound love. Sure, Myla's sporting some wings, pointy ears and evening wear, but I can't find it in me to care. After all the illusions I've been living with, these changes are no biggie.

Myla jogs over to my side. "Ready to kick some ass?"

I smile so hard, my face hurts. "Always."

"Good. I've got a plan. Let's say that arena vow together." She raises her brows. "Aren't you going to warn me how that magic could chain us to the Viking Games for all eternity?"

"Nah. I figure you've got it all worked out."

"How I've missed you." She winks. "On the count of three. 1, 2, 3."

Together, we speak the vow.

We commit our lives to the Viking Games!

Purple sand rises up to surround me. A chill runs across my back. I've seen this change happen so many times, there's no question what's appearing on my skin.

I'm getting the mark for my magical weapon in the Viking Games.

Little by little, the violet particles descend from my body. Turns out, I'm not the only one who's transformed. Where Myla once stood, now there's a massive dragon who doesn't just breathe flame. It *is* fire. The beast takes to the air and swoops above me.

That's Nidhogg, the great Norse dragon. And it's also my wife.

Which means I exactly what marking has just appeared on my skin.

MYLA & LINCOLN

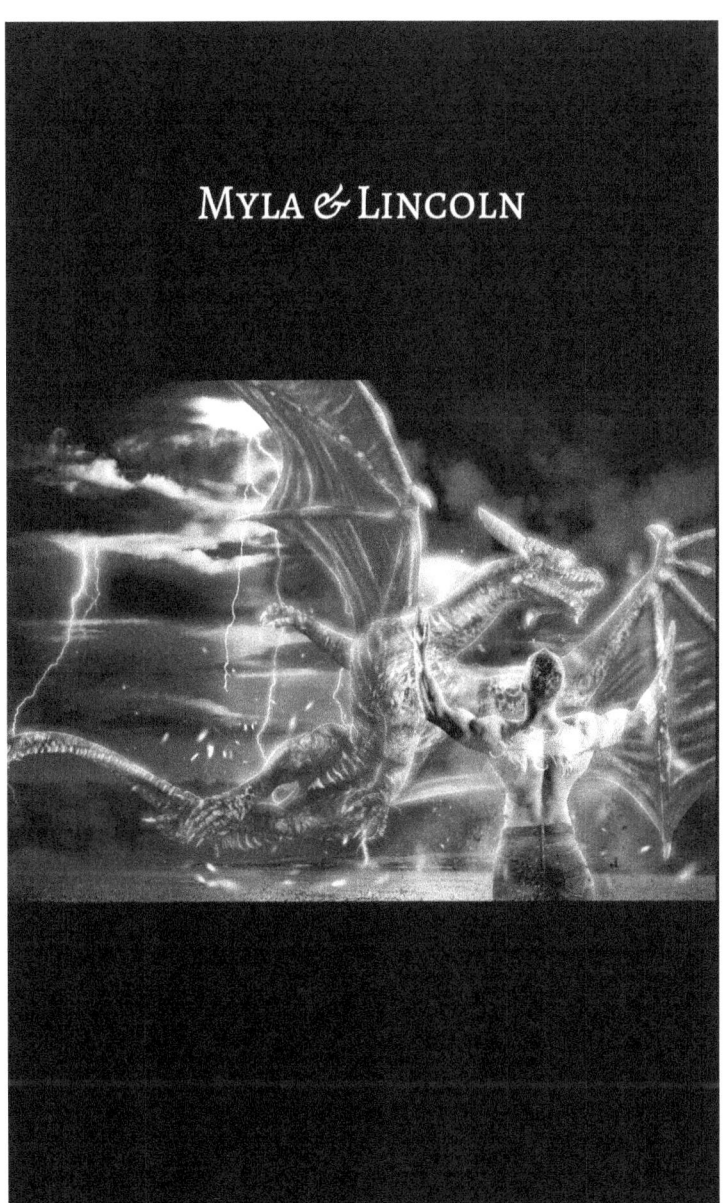

MYLA

*B*eing a dragon is so badass, I can't even. I hover above the arena, careful to choose a spot that's over Fiery Kell's head.

"Hey, Skeletor! How about going back to your own little dimension? Leave me, Lincoln, and our family alone!"

Now, it's the thrax way to give evildoers a chance to back off without getting themselves killed. But in this case, it isn't really a fun option. All of which is why I fly in place and hope Fiery Kell acts like the asshat he is.

The pounding of drums fills the air. Talk about annoying. Fiery Kell lifts his sword. "Now I shall kill you all!"

That's my cue.

I take in a deep breath, feeling the heat grow inside

my chest. Exhaling, I set loose a geyser of flame right at Fiery's Kell's fat face.

The ringmaster doesn't even flinch.

So that sucked.

Lincoln calls to me from the arena floor. "Get his helm!"

I give Fiery Kell another once-over. The closest thing the guy has to an actual helmet is the massive skull he's jammed over his head.

Buh-bye to that.

Swooping down, I clasp the skull thingy in my lower claws and take to the skies. Unfortunately, Kell must have a pretty large head, because both he and his helmet rise from the ground. Someone's a little stuck.

I'm a helper. I can fix this.

Swooping around the arena, I slam Fiery Kell's body into the stands, the floor, and even the balconies. He screams a lot, but that helmet stays put.

Time to get a little gross.

Flying backward, I toss Fiery Kell into the air and set my dragon jaws around his skull helmet. Then I bite down. Hard.

Crack!

The skull helm breaks and Kell returns to his normal size. He also tumbles to the ground at high velocity. I consider flying down to grab him before he hits the earth, but something else grabs my attention instead.

Wow. The stands are all empty and smashed up.

Oops! I forgot to grab Kell.

The ringmaster lands with a thud before Lincoln. I soar down to park by my husband's side.

"Is he alive?" I ask.

Kell gets to his feet and glares in my direction. "How dare you do that to me?"

"Excuse me," I counter. "It's, *how dare you do that to me, oh Queen Dragon Scala.*" I look to Lincoln. "Will you kill him now while I watch?"

My husband gives me one of those looks like I just hung the sun and moon. "Absolutely."

48

LINCOLN

Kell is back to his regular green self. Once again, he does not look pleased.

"You tricked me!" cries the ringmaster. "You made me enter into that agreement with both you and your father... All so you could ruin my perfect arena! You don't really care about your son. Everything centers on your own selfish aims."

Kell pulls a dagger from his utility belt and rushes toward me. When it comes to close combat, one thing remains clear. Kell really does need some professional training.

Perhaps in another life.

As Kell closes in, I ignite my baculum into a long sword and run it straight through his heart. It's a fast death, which is more than this guy deserves. How many lives has he ruined over the centuries with his drums, puppeteering and unbreakable vows? Too many.

The ringmaster falls over, dead. Any loss of life is sad, but with Kell? The more mournful thing is the man he could have been if he'd he'd focused his gifts in a different way.

My thoughts circle back to Maxon. Is my son now free from the ringmaster's spell? I reach into my pocket and pull out Father's runestone. For a moment, the markings glow with magic. Then the rock crumbles into dust.

I exhale. "It's over. The spell on Maxon is broken."

A new female voice booms over the landscape. "Indeed, you have proven yourself worthy."

What happens next is rather surprising. An actual goddess lowers down from the skies. I recognize her immediately from my reading. It is the Norse deity, Idunn.

Dragon Myla waves at her. "Hey, thanks for showing up."

Idunn lands before us. "Did you hear what I said?"

Dragon Myla nods. "Not be to a sore winner, but I already told you I had this nailed."

"I do not speak of you, Myla Lewis." Idunn focuses on me and winks. "Hi, there."

Things rapidly turn awkward with a capital A.

Idunn bats her eyes in my direction. "It was so impressive how you held out against Kell's mind control spells. He used that magic to became the greatest criminal in our Norse Universe. I never thought anyone would stand up to him. Even we deities were afraid."

I bow slightly at the waist. "Thank you for the kind words."

Idunn float-walks closer. "I should very much like to show you my appreciation in private."

Dragon Myla growls and points to her stomach. "Pregnant with his baby here."

I give Idunn my most regal and aloof smile. "I would prefer it if you'd change my wife back to her regular state instead."

"Oh, and while you're at it?" asks Dragon Myla. "If you could send the light elves back to their dimension, that would be super cool."

"There's more," I add. "A number of warriors and ghouls lost their free will to Kell. All of them live under the arena. I would consider it a personal favor if you would restore them, too."

Idunn smiles. "Is that all?"

Dragon Myla shifts her weight. "Since you asked, I was wondering if there's a way to end the morning sickness thing."

"Oh, that just happened because you stood on the

Purple Salient. You'll be fine from here on out." Idunn rubs her palms together. "Since there are no more requests, I guess I have some work to do."

Idunn slams her staff against the ground. Concentric waves of violet power radiate out from the spot. Tendrils of purple magic swirl around the Viking Arena. Stone by stone, the place dissolves into sand.

With the arena gone, the remaining ground bubbles and swirls. One by one, figures rise up from the earth. As each person appears, they flare with purple light and vanish.

I smile. These are the folks who Kell enchanted to live under his arena. Now Idunn is setting them free.

"What will happen to them?" asks Dragon Myla.

"They'll go back to their previous lives," explains Idunn. "And if they don't have anything to return to, then I've always had a soft spot for motherhood and birth. I can help them start new ones."

Once all the residents of the Viking Arena are gone, a fresh set of figures appear. At first, it looks like a bunch of children and one adult. When I look more closely, I count about a hundred light elves. All of them wave frantically at my wife.

"Goodbye, Rustle! Stay safe, Sentinel!" Dragon Myla sniffles. "Stupid hormones."

As before, each elf flares with magic and then disappears.

"Before you ask," says Idunn. "I'm returning them to the Norse Universe." She turns to me and sighs. "It really is a shame, you and me. All the best ones are taken." She slams her staff against the ground once more.

"Now go enjoy your honeymoon!"

HONEYMOON

49

LINCOLN

*T*he next thing I know, Myla and I are back in bed, naked. My wife sleeps while making little snorting noises.

Only we aren't in my private chambers anymore. Idunn has moved us to one of the honeymoon castles in Antrum. My thoughts circle back to four days and a million years ago when I awoke the morning after our wedding and decided I was the luckiest man in the after-realms.

For a long while, I simply watch Myla sleep and soak in the wonder of this moment.

Fortune's favorite again.

—The End—

The adventure continues with ANGELFIRE, Book 5 in the Angelbound Lincoln series

The adventure continues with ANGELFIRE, Angelbound Lincoln #5!

About ANGELFIRE

Someone is making life hell for our favorite royal couple, Lincoln and Myla. Natural disasters have the after-realms falling apart. Humans are going to war left and right. And the hottest couple ever can't find two minutes alone. Sheesh.

The problem? Lincoln's evil brother.

Yes, you read that right. Brother.

Turns out, Lincoln's father was a busy guy in his

youth... and now Connor's secret son, Truman, wants his share of the throne. Even worse, Truman is as awful as Lincoln is noble. When it comes to claiming royal power, nothing stands in Truman's way. Sure, Lincoln is tied by angelic blood to his half brother. But will that connection link them together... or ultimately tear the after-realms apart?

Angelbound Lincoln Series

Stories from the perspective of Mister the Prince

1. Duty Bound
2. Lincoln
3. Trickster
4. Baculum
5. Angelfire

ALSO BY CHRISTINA BAUER

ANGELFIRE

The adventure continues with ANGELFIRE, Angel-bound Lincoln #5!

ANGELBOUND

Experience how it all started with the original ANGEL-BOUND!! Read on for a sample…

FAIRY TALES OF THE MAGICORUM

A modern fairy tale that *USA Today* calls a 'must-read!'
Check out WOLVES AND ROSES!

PIXIELAND DIARIES

PIXIELAND DIARIES tells the story of sassy pixie Calla and 'her' elf prince, Dare.

DIMENSION DRIFT

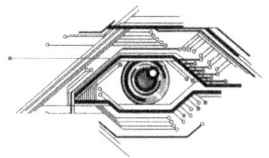

A kick-ass heroine + a swoon-worthy prince + an all-girl heist = SCYTHE!!!

BEHOLDER

Medieval mages ... Slow-burn love ... And heart-pounding action! Check out the BEHOLDER series!

*I*t's been one month, three days, and six hours since I last 'got my gladiator on' and battled in the Arena. Not that I'm obsessing or anything. Sure, I can sneak in and watch someone else fight, but that's a snore.

I roll over on my dingy bed, scooch under the drab covers, and watch the gray drizzle outside my window. Mondays are the pits.

Mom's voice echoes into my bedroom. "Time to get up! You don't want to be late for school, do you, honey?"

I roll my eyes. *Of course,* I want to be late for school.

Raising my head, I open my mouth to say just that, and then decide against it. Instead, I bite my lower lip, yank the pillow over my head and groan. Loudly.

"Don't make noises at me, young lady." Mom rustles

papers in the kitchen. "I've a letter right here. You're on something called the Official Watch List for Unreasonable Tardiness." Her footsteps echo down the hall and pause outside my room. "You'll be suspended from high school at this rate. What do you think about *that?*"

I peep out from under my pillow. Mom looms in my doorway, her fist set on her hip. She's a quasi-demon like me, so she resembles a lovely human with a curvy figure, amber skin, chocolate-brown eyes, and chestnut hair that falls in waves over her shoulders. All quasis have a tail; Mom and I both sport the long and pointed variety. The big differences between us are laugh lines, some grey hair and our opinion of what's 'dangerous' for eighteen-year olds.

I fluff the pillow and slide it under my noggin. Being suspended means no school. Maybe even catching a few Arena matches on the sly. I wag my eyebrows. "And suspension would be bad because?"

"I'd make it that way."

Ugh. She would, too.

Off go my covers. "This is me getting up."

"Good." Mom stomps away.

I shower, pull on some sweats, and sleepwalk into the kitchen, seeing the familiar lime-green appliances, mismatched furniture, and peeling linoleum tile. Everything looks peaceful, quiet, and empty. Another typical

Monday morning before another average day at school. *BO-ring.* I'll have to charm Walker into taking me to the Arena later. Until I'm called to fight again, it's better than nothing.

A thick white envelope sits at the center of the kitchen table. I scoop up and read: "To the Quasi-Demon, Miss Myla Lewis, 666 Dante Row, Purgatory." I lick my thumb and run it over the loopy calligraphy. *Real ink.* My long black tail flicks in a nervous rhythm.

Frowning, I tap the unopened letter against my palm. No one sends me fancy stuff like this. In a blur of motion, my tail darts across my torso, grips the envelope with its arrowhead-shaped end, and tries pulling it from my fingers.

"Hey now!" My tail's always had a mind of its own. For some reason, it's decided this letter is dangerous. I jerk the envelope out of reach, but not before one corner gets totally shredded. "Now, look what you did." My tail slinks behind me to curl guiltily about my ankle.

I reread the outside of the letter. Nothing here to worry about. I *am* a quasi-demon (mostly human with a little demon DNA). I've spent all eighteen years of my life in Purgatory (where human souls get judged for Heaven or Hell, aka the most boring place in the history of ever). This letter's like dozens of others that hit our doorstep each week. Why's my tail on a mission to trash this thing?

I stare at the words again, feeling like they should read: "Open this to turn your life upside-down and your heart into mush."

Clearly, I'm having an off-morning.

I slip the envelope-slash-time-bomb into my mangy backpack. I'll read it later at school.

Mom steps into the kitchen. "How's my sweet baby, Myla-la?" Yes, I'm eighteen years old and Mom still uses pet names from when I was three.

"I'm good." I open a cabinet and pull down a box of Frankenberry cereal.

Mom eyes my every movement, her forehead creasing with worry.

"Did you sleep well last night, Myla?"

Oh, no. Here it comes. I square my shoulders and mentally prepare my 'I'm so very-very caaaaaaalm' voice. "Absolutely." *Nailed it.*

"Any bad dreams?"

"Nope." The 'calm voice' isn't working so well this time.

"Hmm." She taps her cheek. "Met anyone lately? Made any new friends?"

I grit my teeth. All my mornings start off with

maternal interrogations like this one. I find it's best to give soothing, one-word answers. "Negative."

"No friends at all?"

"Only the same one since first grade." I raise my spoon for emphasis. "Cissy."

"That's good." She offers me a shaky grin. "You're safe."

I shoot her a hearty thumbs-up. Today's cross-examination ended relatively quickly; maybe Mom's getting less overprotective. A grin tugs at the corner of my mouth.

"More than safe." I speed-chop the air, karate-style. "I'm a lean, mean, Arena-fighting machine." Wincing, I freeze mid-chop. *How could I be so dumb?* Mom loses her freaking mind whenever I say the word 'Arena.'

There's a pause that lasts a million years while Mom stares at me, her face unreadable. Finally, she moves. But, instead of jumping around in hysterics, she flips about and rifles through cabinets in search of a coffee mug.

Wait a second.

This morning Mom cut her interrogation short *and* she didn't panic when I said the word 'Arena.' I wind my lips into an even-wider grin. Sweeeet. Things *could* be changing, after all.

Leaning back in my chair, I watch Mom pour coffee.

I know she goes overboard because it's just me, her, and this nasty gray ranch house. I have no brothers, sisters, or straight answers about who my father is, except that he's some kind of diplomat. Add it all up and Mom's a wee bit clingy.

Or, at least, she *used* to be. I drum my fingers on the Formica. A less overprotective Mom opens up all sorts of possibilities. I could watch more matches. I could fight in more matches. I could develop interests in things other than the Arena.

Eh, maybe it's a 'no' on that last thing.

Mom slides into the chair across from mine, her large brown eyes watching me through the wisps of steam curling from her mug. "Want a ride to school today? I don't mind waiting outside the door." A muscle twitches at the corner of her eye. "You know, in case anything happens."

My heart sinks to my toes. Then again, maybe Mom's worse than ever.

"Uhhhh." My mouth falls so far open, some Frankenberry rolls off my tongue and onto the tabletop. Did she *really* offer to stand outside school all day long 'in case anything happens?' Cissy told me how parents get extratwitchy during senior year. A shiver rattles my spine. My Mom *plus* 'extra-twitchy' *equals* a huge nightmare.

I force a few deep breaths. "Thanks for the offer." It's

getting really hard to keep my 'calm voice' handy. "I'll pass this time."

Suddenly, the air crackles with energy. A black hole seven feet high and four feet wide appears in the center of the kitchen.

Out of the void steps a ghoul.

My fingers twiddle in his direction. "Hey, Walker." Technically, he's named WKR-7, but I've called him Walker for as long as I can remember.

"Good morning." Walker nods his skull-like head. If he were a few inches taller, the movement would knock his cranium through ceiling, and he's on the short side for a ghoul. It's a mystery how Walker and the rest of the undeadlies handle an eternity of being so crazy-tall.

Walker pulls back his low-hanging hood, showing pale, almost colorless skin and a strong bone structure. He sports the same hairstyle from the day he died: a brush cut with sideburns and no beard. Great black eyes peep at me from deep sockets.

I grin. It's nice to have Walker around. Most ghouls are obsessed with rules and act irritating as Hell. But Walker? He pushes boundaries like a pro, especially when it comes to sneaking me into the Arena. Having him around is like having a cute and somewhat sneaky older brother, only one without a pulse.

"Be careful, Myla." Walker's thin lips droop into a

frown. "That's no way to greet your overlords. I don't mind, but other ghouls could send you to a re-education camp."

I roll my eyes. Purgatory is one massive bureaucracy with the charm of suburbia and the fun of a minimum-security prison. All the work's done by unpaid quasis like me (we're not allowed to call ourselves 'prisoners'). Ghouls keep us in line and make sure we're–*cough, cough*–super happy in our service.

I'm ready to complain about all this to Walker for the millionth time when Mom pipes into the conversation.

"Greetings, my beloved overlord." She's laying it on thick to make up for my sloppy hello. "Want some decaf?" She bows.

Walker nods; ghouls love java.

Mom picks up one of Walker's loopy sleeves, rubbing the fabric between her fingertips. "This is a little thread-bare. Are you here for a new one?" All quasis must perform a service; Mom sews and mends robes. It could be worse. My friend Cissy's mom is a ghoul proctologist.

"No, thank you." Walker eyes the coffee pot greedily.

Mom hands him a full mug marked 'Afterlife's Greatest Ghoul.' Her chocolate eyes nervously scan his face. "What service do you require then?"

Walker frowns. "Myla must battle in the Arena today."

A huge grin spreads across my face. When human souls reach Purgatory, they're given a choice: trial by jury, or trial by combat. Based on the result, they end up either happily floating around Heaven or having their souls consumed in Hell. If the human selects a trial by jury, then it's someone else's problem. But if they choose combat–and the combatant in question is totally evil–then someone like Walker ends up in the kitchen of someone like me. I'm one of a few dozen quasis who kick butt. Literally.

I jump to my feet and clear off my bowl. "Now, this is what I call a Happy Monday."

Mom steps back. "You're sending Myla off to fight today? You can't." She leans against the countertop for support. "Every time she goes, she risks her life." A muscle twitches by her mouth. "Those battles are *to the death*."

I stifle a moan. Mom always focuses on the whole 'to the death' thing like it's the first time she's learned how matches work. Hell, I've battled in the Arena since I was twelve and have yet to get a scratch. You'd think the drama would tone down over the years.

Panting, Mom points to a tattered calendar by the

door. "My little one fought a month ago. She serves once every *three* months, right?"

I raise my hand. "It's not a problem. I'm up for this. Totally."

Mom flashes me a desperate look. "I know that." She grips the countertop like she'll pull it out of the wall. "Please, Walker, tell me it's a mistake."

Walker's black eyes fill with understanding. "Myla must serve today. There's a spike in Arena matches; all fighters have extra battles."

Mom stares at Walker, her jaw grinding out silent rebuttals. After a few moments, she presses her palms to her face, a low sigh escaping her lips. I frown. She's hitting a new level of drama this morning.

Walker shoots me the barest wink. I fight the urge to smile, knowing it means one thing: there's no across-the-boards spike in Arena matches. Purgatory must have an uber-evil soul on their hands, the worst of the absolute worst, and they need their best fighter on it.

That would be me.

Mom shakes her head from side to side. "All those demons and angels. Promise me, you'll keep her away from 'danger.'" She puts special emphasis on the word 'danger.'

"I always do, Camilla."

Mom releases her death-grip from the counter. "Of course."

My back teeth lock. Mom's always going on about protecting me from angels and demons. The demons I understand, but *angels*? Come on.

I zip up my gray hoodie. "Time to trash some evildoers." Stepping to Walker's side, I wait for transport to the Arena.

Mom's hand lightly touches her throat. "Be safe!"

"I'll be super-safe, don't you worry."

"And don't be late for school."

I slap on a smile. "On it, Mom."

Walker bows his head. "Stand back, I'll summon a portal." A new black hole appears in the center of the kitchen. I glance into the darkness, feeling the Frankenberry in my belly come up for a repeat performance. Using a portal feels like tumbling through empty space with a killer case of the stomach flu. Helpful safety tip: hold a ghoul's hand or you'll fall forever.

Taking a deep breath, I grab Walker's chilly fingers so tightly, I'd cut off his blood flow, if he had any. Together, we step into the portal, topple through nothingness, and walk out again onto the sandy earth of the Arena floor. I try my best to look ready-for-battle instead of ready-to-puke.

Walker offers me a sympathetic glance. "Shall we find a place to sit?"

"Nah, I'm fine, thanks." I scan the open-air stadium around me. The Arena's a nasty old ruin, all chipped gray rock and busted sandstone columns. How the place stays upright is a total mystery. The fighting floor is one huge uneven clod of dirt, the bleachers are basically rubble, and the entire top level looks ready to collapse.

I freaking love it here.

The stands lie open and empty, except for a few quasis. They're all fighters like me, trying to catch someone else's match. Mom used to attend too, but all the moaning and gasping got so out of hand, she was banned ages ago. I can't say I was bummed. Nothing like having your Mom yell 'Baby, don't diiiiiiiiiiiiiiiie' when you're twelve and fighting a demon for the first time.

A gravelly voice echoes through the air. "Greetings, *slave.*" The word 'slave' is said with particular venom.

Every muscle in my body goes on alert. I'd know that voice anywhere, and I absolutely loathe its owner. I scrape lint from under my fingernails and pretend not to notice the seven-foot tall ghoul looming behind me.

Walker steps between us. "Greetings, SKE-12."

My mouth winds into a mischievous grin. "Hey, Sharkie.'" SKE-12 hates his nickname, so I work it into every encounter.

Sharkie frowns. "My name is SKE-12, *slave.*"

Walker sets his hand on my shoulder, gently guiding me so I stand face-to-navel with Sharkie, master of Arena ceremonies and all-around dickhead. He hasn't changed a bit since my last match, not that ghouls often do. He's gray-skinned with large coal-black eyes, a skull-like hole for a nose, and teeth that have been filed to tiny points. His long silver robes hang in tatters; a tall black staff is gripped in his bony hand.

Walker gives my shoulder a squeeze. "Myla was just about to greet her ghoul overlord properly, weren't you, Myla?" Standing next to Sharkie, even Walker looks vertically challenged.

"My bad." I bow extra-low. "Greetings, SKE-12."

His buggy black eyes narrow into slits. Sharkie always knows when I'm making fun of him, and it drives him crazy. "I'll have no mischief from you today."

I bow again, even lower this time. "Yes, I'm fresh out."

Sharkie turns to Walker, his black eyes flaring bright red. "Control her." His gaze swings back to me. "We've an especially evil human soul fighting today. I hope to watch you die at last."

I pick something off my molar with my pinky. "I'm sure you do."

Sharkie steps closer, his pointy teeth click-clacking

as he speaks. "The soul you fight today is so evil, the angels have begged the Great Scala to stand by, ready to transport him to Hell the moment he's defeated. Which will never happen." He leans in closer. "You. Are. Doomed."

My brows pop up. Normally, the Scala migrates tons of souls at once in what's called an iconigration. For this guy to get solo treatment, he must be a SUPER nasty. *Fun.* "Bring it on, Shar–."

Walker grabs my elbow. "Look, Myla! Your friends are here!" He points across the stadium floor. "We must depart." He bows once more to Sharkie. "Excuse us." As we speed-walk away, Walker whispers in my ear. "If I weren't already dead, I'd have had a heart attack just now."

"Eh, Sharkie's harmless."

"Because I placate him for you." He shoots me a sly look. "Why must you always taunt him?"

"Not sure." I shrug. "It's a hobby." A few yards ahead stands a ghoul named XP-22, and a hovering green blob that's Sheila, the Limus demon.

I shoot Sheila a friendly wave. "Hey Shiel, how are the kids?" Sheila's nice, so long as you don't stand close enough for her to swallow you whole. XP-22, on the other hand, is a total drip. I don't even glance in his direction.

"The kids are good, Myla, getting bigger every day… Just like you." Sheila's entire body shivers, which is a little scary since she's six feet tall, three feet wide, and has fourteen red eyes the size of tennis balls. "It seems like yesterday you were twelve and about to fight your first demon." Her huge gaping mouth twists into a grin. "How old are you now, honey?"

"Eighteen."

A blob-like arm stretches out from Sheila's side, lengthening into a gooey hand with eighteen long fingers. "Almost grown up! Have you been assigned your service yet?" 'Assigning your service' is ghoul-speak for locking a quasi into a life-long job after high school. We're not allowed to call it 'prison labor.' I shiver. There are some mighty foul careers out there too, like the infamous anal probe development lab.

Before I can reply to Sheila's question, Sharkie thumps his staff against the ground.

"Attention!" Sharkie raises his arms, his ragged gray robes swaying in slow, ghostly motions. Beneath his huge hood, his eyes shine as two points of red light.

Sheila waves her eighteen-fingered hand in my direction. "Well, what'll your service be? Port-a-Potty Squad? Greeter at Ghoul-Mart?"

Pointing to Sharkie, I make a 'sh' face to Sheila. It's rude to talk once the ceremony starts, plus I hate answering the whole 'what'll your service be' question. Sheila nods and oozes away. Bonus.

THUD. THUD. THUD. THUD. Sharkie thumps his staff four more times. "I bring you the Oligarchy!"

Four ghouls in scarlet robes appear along the top tier of the stadium, one at each point of the compass. Called the Oligarchy, they rule Purgatory as one collective mind, and a not-so-creative mind too, based on how they name ghouls.

In one motion, the Oligarchy close their eyes, bow their gray heads, and open a series of massive portals around the lip of the stadium. Angels and demons appear in the dark openings, and then stream down the uneven stone steps in one great wave.

The angels take their seats in an orderly line, their bodies coming in many shapes, sizes and colors. All have massive white wings, floor-length linen robes, little open-toed sandals, and eyes that glow with an unearthly blue light. They can hide their wings if they want to, but they keep them out for important occasions, like watching Arena fights.

In other words, angels are cool.

On the other side of the stadium, the demons move in a frenzied pack, roaring in a mad rush for the best seats. Large, furry creatures stomp along next to small and slimy monsters. Tiny, spiked demons zoom above their heads. Eye color is all they share in common: black stands for 'neutral' while red means 'run for the hills.'

As I watch them scramble over each other, my head shakes from side to side. Demons are cool too, but only when I get to kill them.

The lively hum of stadium chatter collapses into anxious silence.

She is coming.

I scan the top level of the Arena. The four great portals stand empty and dark. Acting in unison, the Oligarchy ghouls lower their heads. A low hum fills the air. Pale yellow light glimmers in the eastern portal; all eyes turn in that direction. A figure in white appears in the darkened entryway. My breath catches.

This is Verus, Queen of the Angels.

She stands willowy and tall with long black hair, high cheekbones, and exotic, almond-shaped eyes. She's timeless, beautiful, and more than a little bit frightening. Sometimes she watches me so carefully during matches, it gives me the creeps.

Beside her stands a short-ish ghoul with a handsome face, square jaw, and large black eyes.

I elbow Walker in the ribs. "That guy could be your brother."

He looks up, smiles. "You don't say."

"I did say." I glance at him out of my right eye. "So, is he?"

"You know your mother doesn't allow me to share personal information." He shoots me a sympathetic smile. "Take it up with her later." He clears his throat and rocks a bit on his heels. "When I'm not around, if you don't mind."

My 'why don't you tell me anything' fights with Mom are nothing short of legend. I stick out my tongue at Walker. "Fine. I will."

Verus steps onto her balcony, a small entourage behind her. As she slips into a white stone throne, the stadium's silence is ripped apart by howls and screeches. A new outline appears in the western portal: Armageddon, the King of Hell. He's tall and lanky with black onyx skin that's smooth as polished stone. A blade-like nose divides his long face, ending in a pointed chin. He scans the stadium, his eyes blazing as two searing points of scarlet light. A shiny black tuxedo hugs his wiry frame.

Unholy Hell. Every nerve ending in my body goes on alert. While Verus is a wee bit scary, Armageddon gives off a 'greater demon' aura. If you get too close (which has happened to me more than once), every cell in your body shudders with terror. But that's not what *really* gets me about the King of Hell. Most demons are short-term thinkers. They want to kill your body and eat your soul, end of story. Not Armageddon. He planned for years to take over both Hell and Purgatory. That kind of craftiness brings evil to a new level.

Armageddon saunters away from the portal, a large entourage of gorilla-like Manus demons behind him. The Oligarchy collapse onto their knees as he passes by, their movements reminding me of marionettes whose strings are cut. Their deep voices echo through the stadium. "We praise thee, Great King." The ghouls may rule us in name, but everyone knows who *really* runs the show.

Without so much as a glance toward the Oligarchy, Armageddon speeds onto the balcony across from Verus, his entourage close behind him. The King of Hell slips into his own black stone throne.

Sharkie thumps his staff again. "Ghouls, demons, and angels!" The stadium falls silent.

I glance at my watch and grin. Right now, I should be in homeroom.

With a flourish of his bony arm, Sharkie gestures to the four scarlet-robed ghouls standing along the stadium's top level. "Today, the Oligarchy bring you a spectacle of governing efficiency: an Arena battle to the death witnessed by the magnificent leader of our joint troops in the Ghoul Wars...The acclaimed liberator of all Purgatory...Armageddon!"

The demons positively lose their freaking minds in a deafening cheer. My upper lip twists. *Screw Armageddon and his fake liberation of Purgatory. He handed us over to ghouls so we'd send more souls to Hell, pure and simple.* It's only when demon DNA mixes with a human that you get different powers. On their own, demons are mindless soul-munchers. My eyes flare red. I start to make a lewd hand gesture in Armageddon's direction, but Walker snags my wrist before I get too far. He shoots me a stern look, mouthing the words 'put a lid on it, Lewis.'

Nodding, I grip my hands behind my back. I'm enough of a warrior to know he's right: taunting Armageddon is a B-A-D idea. I focus on the ground, force myself to breathe slowly, and try to keep my cool. My inner demon has a mind of its own with more than my tail. When my eyes flare red, it's my demonic side getting rowdy. Sometimes, it's a struggle to keep it in check.

From his great stone throne, Armageddon watches the frenzied demon crowd, his thin red lips curling upwards. He scans every face, soaking in each expression and nuance, weaving them all into some complex and dark plan.

I shiver. He's being crafty again, and damn, that makes my skin crawl.

Raising his hand, Armageddon quiets the crowd. "Today's soul was a favorite of mine on earth. Unbelievable strength. No capacity for conscience. Pure untainted evil. When he wins this battle—which he will, make no mistake—then we'll finally have one of our own inside the gates of Heaven." The dark seats howl with glee while the angels collectively shiver. Grinning, Armageddon retakes his seat.

All faces turn to the Angel Verus. She slowly rises to her feet, her white wings spreading regally behind her. She shouts one word: "NEVER!" The force of her yell sets columns rattling and rubble tumbling to the ground. Her gaze turns to me, eyes flashing bright. Armageddon follows suit, his irises glowing red as he scans me from head to toe. A satisfied smirk winds the corner of his mouth. I've seen that look on other faces; it's the one that says '*that* little girl? Maybe she's won before, but against *this* opponent? Are you serious?'

Which pisses me off, big time.

Sharkie thumps his staff again; a human soul appears nearby. In life, this ghost was a man about six feet tall with broad shoulders and two-hundred fifty pounds of solid muscle beneath them. Now he appears as a spectral version of his mortal self: a ghostly hulk whose pale body looks ready to burst from his faded jeans and dirty white t-shirt.

Sharkie addresses the spirit. "Vincent Francis Morris, you've chosen trial by combat, is this true?"

"The Choker. My name's...The Choker." Squinting his piggish eyes, the ghost flicks a fat tongue over his full lips.

"I will ask again." Sharkie's irises flare bright red. "Have you chosen trial by combat?"

The ghost curls his hands into fists. "Yes, combat."

"Select your opponent." Sharkie grins, his knife-like teeth glimmer in the pale light. "First, we offer XP-22."

The Choker eyes our 'fighting ghoul.' With barely-there skin and the muscle tone of toilet paper, anyone could crush XP-22. In fact, the Choker would probably snap him in three seconds or less, but I don't think he'll choose to. Ghouls look mighty terrifying, even the weak ones. Most humans avoid them.

The Choker is no different. "I'll pass."

Sharkie moves his thin arm to the next figure in line. "Second, we offer Sheila, the Limus demon."

Sheila's fourteen red eyes whip about her upper body, finally stopping to glare at the ghostly human. She stretches wide the black hole that serves as her mouth, letting out a gurgling roar. When that girl puts her game on, she's terrifying.

"Hmm." The Choker's beady eyes give Sheila a long stare; the entire Arena seems to hold its breath.

I glance at Sheila and shake my head. Limus demons are almost as easy to kill as XP-22. The trick is, they're super-flammable. One match and you turn a six-foot monster into a puddle of harmless goo. But like XP-22, they look worse than they actually fight.

The Choker frowns. "Nope."

"And third, we offer the quasi-demon, Myla."

The Choker's eyes slowly scan me from head to toe, his creepy gaze lingering on the curves under my t-shirt and sweats. Rage shoots up my spine. What a scumbag. If he stopped thinking with his pants for two seconds, he'd notice my demon tail instead of my boobs and butt. Some quasis get stuck with pig- or bunny-bottoms, but I hit the jackpot: the long and thin variety with an arrowhead end. Even better, it's coated in dragon scales, so the thing's nearly impossible to block or cut.

But the Choker isn't being smart. He stares into my big watery brown eyes and long lashes; I shamelessly blink in fake-terror. For trial by combat to be valid, the soul must have a chance at winning. They get three options, two of which are relatively easy to defeat. Then, there's me, the one nobody should pick. Except they always do.

"I choose her." His thick mouth stretches into a

vicious smile. "I'll fight Myla." In a low voice, he adds: "You'll find out why they call me the Choker."

I jam my hands in my pockets and fake-shiver. And you'll find out why they called me to fight you, dickhead.

Sharkie thumps his staff on the ground again, and the ghostly Choker turns into two-hundred fifty pounds of real human. "So be it."

—End of Sample—

Order ANGELBOUND today!

APPENDIX I - THE USUAL

Christina Bauer thinks that fantasy books are like bacon: they just make life better. All of which is why she writes romance novels that feature demons, dragons, wizards, witches, elves, elementals, and a bunch of random stuff that she brainstorms while riding the Boston T. Oh, and she includes lots of humor and kick-ass chicks, too. Christina lives in Newton, MA with her husband, son, and semi-insane golden retriever, Ruby.

Stalk Christina on Social Media

Blog:
http://monsterhousebooks.com/blog/
category/christina

Facebook:
https://www.facebook.com/authorBauer/

Instagram:
https://www.instagram.com/christina_cb_bauer/

Twitter:
@CB_Bauer

VLOG:
https://tinyurl.com/Vlogbauer

Web site:
www.bauersbooks.com

IF YOU ENJOYED THIS BOOK...

...Please consider leaving a review, even if it's just a line or two. Every bit truly helps, especially for those of us who don't *write by the numbers,* if you know what I mean. Plus I have it on good authority that every time you review an indie author, somewhere an angel gets a mocha latte. For reals.

And angels need their caffeine, too.

ACKNOWLEDGMENTS

If you're reading my freaking acknowledgements, chances are, I should thank you for something. So, for the record: you are awesome, dear reader.

That said, huge and heartfelt thanks must go out to my husband and son for their rock-solid support. Writing books means a lot of early mornings, late nights, long weekends, and never-ending patience. You two are the best guys in the universe, period.

After that, I must thank the extensive network of reviewers, friends and colleagues who helped me build my writing chops in general. Gracias.

Finally, deep affection goes out to my late, much loved, and dearly missed Aunt Sandy and Uncle Henry. You saw the writer in me, always. Thank you, first and last.

SUBSCRIBE

Get a FREE copy of Christina Bauer's novella, BEVERLY HILLS VAMPIRE, when you sign up for her personal newsletter:

https://tinyurl.com/bauersbooks

Not available in stores

BEVERLY HILLS VAMPIRE

A NOVELLA BY
CHRISTINA BAUER

APPENDIX II - AUTHOR THOUGHTS

*D*ear Readers,
     Since you're here at the end of the book, I thought you might want some extra insights on writing this book. Here goes!

Send Out The Evil Clowns

Originally, I did not have a Norse theme for the games. It was more of a circus thing. And the handlers were all evil-looking clowns (who are actually super nice). I even had Harvey, a seemingly evil clown that befriended Myla. Then one day over breakfast, my husband saw the following image for the clown in question.

HARVEY

My husband almost choked on his bagel. I decided that including the evil clown might not be a great idea. One of the fights did include a Nordic creature, so I played around with extending that Viking myth to the whole fighting circuit. The Fighting Circus became the Viking Games, and it worked much better to have an alternate arena experience to contrast Myla's life. So the evil clowns met the delete key.

Seeing Each Other Before

In the book, Myla and Lincoln 'see' each other before they actually meet. This is based on my own experience.

Both my husband and I grew up in Buffalo, NY--a place that's basically one big room. After we started dating, we figured out that we'd attended some of the same events over the years. In a few cases, I even noticed him, mostly because he was either singing or making out with his then-girlfriend. So that experience worked its way into this book as well.

Side Note: The then-girlfriend later invited my husband to her own wedding. I offered to go as his plus one and look fabulous. My husband wisely decided he was too busy to attend.

What's The Deal With Connor?

If you want the full explanation for why Connor is such a freak about all things related to the King of Hell, there's more explanation in ARMAGEDDON (Angel-bound Origins Book 7).

Enjoy!

-CB

HAPPILY EVER BEGINNINGS

*I*n Western culture, many of our fairy tales end with, *and lived happily ever after.* That's not the case in the East, where myths often begin with, *once upon a time, a hero and heroine got married...*

When I first learned this, it blew my fucking mind.

Ever since then, I've been obsessed with the idea of a lost canon of storytelling that focuses on adventures in the *happily ever after.* In BACULUM, I try to explore what happens to a couple when a big change comes into your joint life. In the book, the transformation comes in the form a new baby, but it could be a new career, college, you name it.

In this story, the magic of the Nine Realms represents how chaos can pull you away from your true self during upheaval. The power of a strong relationship is that it can act as true North in terms of guiding your inner compass.

Readers sometimes ask how many stories I plan to tell about Myla and Lincoln. I honestly don't know. There are a lot of books that focus on an overall arc of falling in love.Based on my own reading, that storyline can last between one and five books before it starts to fray. At some point, the reader is like, *hook up or shut up!*

Time to put on my reader hat here. I haven't yet found a similar body work for stories about couples where there's a different arc in each installment. I do find ones with a *monster of the week* style, which I adore. But that doesn't haver as much impact unless it's paired with an emotional journey. I find that I need to pull these arcs out of my ass. Here's the journey through the Lincoln series:

Book 1. DUTY BOUND - prequel novella to set up Lincoln's character and world

Book 2. LINCOLN - our hero falls in love

Book 3. TRICKSTER - Lincoln realizes what it means to really support his strong female partner while staying a powerhouse in his own right

Book 4. BACULUM - a new baby is on the way! Lincoln struggles with this change and related fears he'll become his father

Book 5. ANGELFIRE - Lincoln discovers he has a half-brother who is a shit bag... but also had a lot more fun growing up. Lincoln confronts the "revenge of the unlived life" as Robertson Davies outlines it in FIFTH BUSINESS.

Long story short, if you ask me how many Lincoln and Myla stories out there, I have no idea. Over the years, I've learned not to ask too many questions about how Writer Me functions.

I'm just glad she works so hard in return for hot mochas and cool new fairy tales.

*I*t's tricky to write about someone else's sacred text as a myth. As <u>Joseph Campbell</u> said, 'myths are *other people's religion'* (my emphasis, not Campbell's). That said, I'd like to share three mind-opening things about the *Ramayana*, a Hindu epic myth that's a sacred text to millions. It's the first story I read that began with a hero and heroine were married instead of ending with that idea.

Mind = blown.

In turn, that revelation started a lifelong obsession that basically says, hey, where the fuck are all the stories that start with two people getting together? Over the years, the result has been the many Lincoln-Myla stories.

But I digress.

Back to the Ramayana.

SUMMARY: the *Ramayana* (loosely translated as 'Rama's Journey') is the story of King Rama's odyssey to rescue his wife Sita after she's abducted by Ravana. The book is really-really-really long and that's a crazy-short synopsis, but there you go.

As an author and myth junkie (I've written before about Isis, Athena and Cinderella), this story blew my mind for four reasons:

1. How The Tale Begins

I really can't hit this point too hard. In the West, most fables *end* with 'they were married and lived happily ever after.' Not the case here. The *Ramayana* basically *begins* with 'Rama and Sita were married, and so started their adventure.' When I first read this, I was stunned. It never occurred to me that marriage would be the *beginning* of an epic myth. Western fables focus on courting and falling in love... so what are we missing out on here? I'm still working on the answer to that question, BTW.

2. The Super-Cute Romance Between Rama and Sita

As a Westerner, I thought we cornered the market on

love stories. In the *Ramayana*, there are charming passages with Rama and Sita hanging out in a garden, all googly for each other.

3. A baddie who was...too good?

We already covered how Ravana abducted Sita. Now, depending on the version of the *Ramayana* you read, Ravana may have had a legit grudge against Rama and reason to grab Sita. That said, what struck me in reading the *Ramayana* is that Ravana's real problem was the following: he was a good guy who went to extremes. He had the most lovely city, most learned scholars, and loudest prayers. To me, it seemed like he wanted the most beautiful Sita to complete his 'perfection set.' And come on, we all know someone like this, right?

Hell, I've been that person sometimes.

Westerners often celebrate extremists as non-conformists and true individuals who really push the envelope. But extremists are also the group who---whatever other labels you put on them---are the most likely to cause some seriously huge trouble. Personally, I think that's why Ravana is always pictures with multiple heads. Even in that, he's extreme.

4. Becoming the Monster

This my totally personal interpretation here, but in fighting Ravana, Rama has the challenge of becoming the same extremist dick that he fought against. It's a long journey for Rama to save Sita, and things change along the way. It reminds me of that famous quote:

"Beware that, when fighting monsters, you yourself do not become a monster... for when you gaze long into the abyss, the abyss gazes also into you."
- Friedrich W. Nietzsche

Conclusion

So there you have it: the story that launched a thousand story ideas for Lincoln and Myla!